NOT of This World

Jessica LeeAnn

After The Storm Publishing
GO THROUGH TO GET THROUGH...THE STORM

ISBN-13: 978-0692741313
ISBN-10: 0692741313

AFTER THE STORM PUBLISHING, LLC
A Division of Peace in the Storm Publishing, LLC
39 Myrtle Avenue #2
North Plainfield, NJ 07060

Visit our Website at
www.afterthestormpublishing.com

DEDICATION

I dedicate this book to my amazing Mom, my awesome daughter, Da'Mya, my favorite person in the world, Nesha, and my beautiful Grandmother. I appreciate and cherish each and every one of you. Your presence in my life means the world to me! Love you much!

Acknowledgments

I want to acknowledge each and every person who has read my blogs, poems, short stories and self-published books. Your support has not gone unnoticed. I want to acknowledge and give a special thanks to Sharel, Elissa, and the entire After the Storm Publishing family for believing in my gift and giving me the platform to share it with the world. Last, but definitely not least, I want to acknowledge my Divine Creator, the Most High God, for blessing me with the talent of writing and the courage to share my gift.

One

Today is the first day of work at my new job and I'm so excited. I felt like a naïve kid starting high school for the first time. I'm finally getting my fresh start in life and I can't wait to see how my life will change. I have been praying and fasting for a blessing and it's finally here. I'm so happy to start a new job. I've worked at my last job as a waitress for six years and I've finally found a new career. While waitressing, I went back to school and got my master's and I can't wait to put my new degree to use. I'll be meeting new people, learning new skills, and making more money. Most importantly, I will never have to take anyone's order ever again in life. I appreciate having a job but I don't ever want to waitress again in my life. I would have gotten my degree years ago, but I stayed home to help out with my grandmother after she completed chemo. I spent most of my early twenties being a nurse without a degree. I'm grateful that my grandmother is cancer-free so I can live my own life.

I wiped the crust from my eyes and sat on my bed with my head down, silently thanking God for this day. My phone buzzed with a reminder that I needed to leave soon so that I can make it to San Francisco in time. I checked and double checked my outfit in the mirror one last time before I headed out of the door. I hope that I look professional enough for Mr. Whitmore. When I interviewed with him, he was dressed so nicely. Then I remembered that the women in the office were walking around in nice business suits, cute dresses and stilettos. I suddenly felt less confident in my black pantsuit, polka dot collared shirt and black flats. I didn't have any extravagant outfits in my closet to change into so, this pantsuit will just have to do.

I hopped in my car and headed over to the Bart station and prayed that I wouldn't miss my stop once I boarded. I was so nervous that I didn't listen to any music on the ride to the MacArthur station. My nerves were pretty bad at the moment. I usually meditate, read a chapter or two in the bible and a daily devotional in the mornings, but I didn't get a chance to today so I'll catch up on the Word at lunch. I don't want to read on the Bart because I needed to pray that my nerves won't make a fool of me.

I finally made it to the Bart station and eagerly made my way to the platform. I smiled at people, but of course no one returned the smile. After all, it's early and they don't know me. I stood on the platform waiting for my train to arrive, trying to silently speak some confidence to myself. I felt my phone vibrate with a text message. It was from my sister, Hannah. She told me to have a good day and included one of my favorite scriptures, Jeremiah 29:11. I smiled, replied and thanked my sister. By the time I finished replying to Hannah my train had arrived.

The ride to San Francisco was quicker than I thought. When I made it to the building I'll be working in, I felt a sense of peace come over me. God was answering those prayers I sent up asking for peace, and as usual, He provided it to me right on time. I went up to my floor and plastered a huge smile on my face. I was excited and not as nervous as I was when I left my house.

The receptionist had her head down as I approached her desk, so I cleared my throat to get her attention.

"Excuse me, hi, good morning. My name is Tamar Hall. I'm here for Mr. Richard Whitmore. It's my first day as his executive assistant."

"Good for you. Have a seat. I'll let him know you're here." The receptionist never looked me in my face. She dialed three digits on her phone, told Mr. Whitmore I was here and placed her attention back on her monitor. She had china bangs, round eyes, a cute button nose and full lips. She was too beautiful to be so rude.

A few moments later Mr. Whitmore walked out from behind the glass doors with an intense look on his face and I became nervous again. He's a tall, brown skinned man with a thick beard. His suit was very nice and it looked very expensive. "Ms. Hall, good to see you again."

"Good to see you too, Mr. Whitmore."

"Come on, let's get you started."

"Okay." I followed Mr. Whitmore to his wing of the building.

"How was your commute to work?" he asked, as they walked towards his office. Where are they walking to?

"It was good, not too bad."

"You took Bart, right?"

"Yes, I did."

"Good. Going forward HR will be funding your transportation. You'll fill all of that paperwork out before you leave today."

"Great, thanks."

"Go ahead and put your things here on this desk. This will be your area. Go over the forms on your desk. Once you're done, bring them to me and we can go over your agenda for the day. Cool?"

"Yes, that's cool."

"Great, see you in a bit."

Mr. Whitmore walked into his office and left me to figure out what I needed to do. I filled out the typical paperwork any new hire has to fill out and logged into my computer with the information he left with me. My username and password for everything was in a manila folder. I logged into all of the software listed to make sure that everything worked. Once I was done with that, I grabbed the notebook that was sitting on my desk and went into Mr. Whitmore's office. I tapped on the door before entering.

"Mr. Whitmore. I'm all done with my paperwork. What's next?"

"Let's go over your expectations. Have a seat."

"Okay."

"So I would like for you to be here by 8:45 every morning to get coffee started for me; I'm here at nine sharp every morning and I like to have my coffee first thing when I arrive. I have you on my email list so reply to all of the ones that you have an answer for. Leave the ones you can't answer and move them into the folder in my inbox labeled urgent. Everything else can wait until I have time. Type up all of my voicemail messages along with my meetings for the day and place them on my desk in a manila folder. Take messages for anyone who calls me, even if I'm here.

You'll be attending every meeting that I have in the building and I expect for you to take thorough notes. Type them up and email them to me when the meeting is over. When I have to meet with clients, you are responsible for making sure they have a typed agenda along with a notepad and pen to take notes in the conference room. Is that clear so far?"

"Yes, but I have one question. Do I really need to fix your coffee for you every morning?"

"Will that be a problem?"

"No, it just surprises me that you don't go to Starbucks or the coffee shop next door."

"No, I don't drink Starbucks so I'll be expecting hot coffee when I get here. Understood?"

"Sure understood."

"Good. You will also have access to my calendar. Look at it and get prepared for the meetings I have booked for today and tomorrow. Make it a habit going forward. I won't remind you to do so. If you have any questions, ask me this week. I'll expect for you to figure everything else out on your own starting next week. Clear?"

"Yes. Yes, very clear."

"Thank you, Tamar. I'm excited to have you here. Let's get to work."

"Thank you. Mr. Whitmore. I'm very grateful for this opportunity."

"Very well."

I went back to my desk and let out a quiet sigh. I have a lot to adjust to and rather quickly. Mr. Whitmore is very demanding I see. I'm going to try my best not to be intimidated by his persona. He seems cocky, spoiled and entitled. I can't believe he actually wants me to make his coffee.

I typed up everything I wrote down in our meeting and started organizing the rest of my day and the following day as instructed. While all of the things Mr. Whitmore said was a bit overwhelming, I was still pretty excited to work for him.

The rest of the day went by pretty smoothly. I attended two meetings, typed up the notes I took and emailed them to Mr. Whitmore. I studied his calendar for the rest of the week just to be two steps ahead of the game. We have a meeting to attend at ten the next morning so I went ahead and prepped for that.

It seems like I'll be mostly answering the phone, taking messages, replying to emails, attending meetings and taking notes. Luckily I don't have to attend his off-site meetings. I'll be receiving notes from whatever assistant that will be at those meetings via email. I'm responsible for making sure they are available to him by the time he gets back.

The rest of the week went by fairly quickly. I caught on pretty fast and seemed to not be a nuisance to Mr. Whitmore. So far he's easy to get along with. He comes in every morning at nine, I have his Columbian coffee ready along with his notes and messages and he's pleased. I noticed that he always says 'good morning', he dresses extremely well, yells my name if he needs something urgent and quietly do whatever it is that he does when he's in his office. He spends a lot of time emailing, on the phone and in meetings. When he's not doing either of those things, he's asking me to research things for him.

So far, things were going well for me at my new job. I haven't met any of the other ladies on a personal level, but I see them all day strutting in five inch heels, perfect make-up and designer dresses. I'm not the type of woman to play dress up so I feel very uncomfortable when I pass them in the office. I have to remind myself not to compare myself to them. I'm here to work, not compete.

Anyway, I was so grateful to finally have a job that I deemed respectable. I've been going to church these last few

Sunday's with praise and worship in my heart and joy in my soul because I was so happy that God opened this door for me.

When I received my first check, I was even more grateful and shocked when I heard the balance in my checking account. I knew how much I'd be making, but it's so much different when you know the money is in your account. I was so excited about my first check that I called my sister after work so that we could celebrate.

"Hannah, what are you doing tonight?"

"Um, let's see; being a wife. What do you think I'm doing?"

"See if Mark will watch the kids for a couple of hours so that we can go out and have dinner. I got my first check today and it's big."

"Hey! That's great. Congratulations! Okay, I'll ask the hubby and call you back. Can we eat some steak?"

"Yes, Hannah, we can have steak."

"Well yes, I'm definitely going. So count me in. If Mark won't watch them, then his mom will. What time are you picking me up?"

"I'll be there at seven."

"It's a date, sis!"

I hung up with my sister and squealed. I was so happy to finally earn some decent money making it possible for me to finally move out of my grandmother's house and live like an adult. I appreciate being able to live with my grandmother for as long as she allows me to, but I'm ready to be on my own.

I said a quick prayer before I closed down the office and headed to the Bart station. I put my earbuds in and cranked up the volume on my I-pod. Travis Greene was singing his heart out in my ears and I let his anointed voice take me to a place of worship as I rode the Bart back to Oakland.

When I made it to Hannah's house, I had to laugh when I saw her. She got all dressed up like I was really taking her on a date. I shook my head at my sister as she strutted to my car in a pair of black boots. She looked really cute.

"Girl, what do you have on?"

"My date night boots. Isn't this a date?" she asked.

"No, not really; more like a celebration for me. I'm the one who should be dressed up."

"Well I didn't know you were going to come in your work clothes. I thought you were going to get fly with me."

"Negative."

"Whatever. I'm not changing. Let's roll."

We headed over to the House of Prime Rib to pig out. Once we arrived to the quaint restaurant, we were greeted by a petite hostess with short, dark hair and glasses. There was a twenty minute wait so Hannah and I chatted with the older couple who was also waiting to be seated. A tall, thin guy with blonde hair finally called our names to be seated and we obediently followed him to our seats.

After ordering our drinks, I told my sister all about my new job, my demanding boss and the women who work there.

"I'm telling you, Hannah, they're all beautiful. You'd think they were all models."

"So? We're beautiful, too."

"Not their kind of beautiful though."

"Interesting. Do you feel out of place?"

"Yeah, I do. You know I'm not into dressing fly, wearing make-up and wearing fancy hairstyles. I like wearing my pantsuits and rocking my natural hair. I can't see myself going to work in high heels and skirts. That's only for church. Well, not the ones they wear, but you know what I mean."

"Well, keep being yourself. You were hired just as you are, so there's no need to try and change yourself now."

"I'm not, it's just a little intimidating being around women so beautiful and I'm just so regular."

"What are you talking about, girl? You're gorgeous! And you are not just regular, you are saved and sanctified. The only difference is that you're a woman of the Most High and you respect your body as the temple it is, as you should. Forget about those shallow heffa's."

"Yeah, you're right. So tell me about Mark's new business?"

Hannah and I chatted about her husband's new business venture. He opened two laundromats in Richmond and was doing pretty well. I was so proud of him.

I remember when they first got together. They were too cute! They met at church and he was smitten with Hannah from day one. He chased her for two years before she went out with him and a year later he proposed. A year and a half after that they were married and pregnant with my niece. Seven years and two kids later, they're still going strong. I'm so happy for my sister. She did everything the right way and waited for her Boaz. She saved her virginity for her first night as a wife, enjoyed being a newly-wed couple and then had a baby. I'm going to be just like her when I get my life together.

After I dropped Hannah back off at home, I went to my grandmother's house and crashed in my room. I lay on the bed looking up at the ceiling with a smile on my face. I could feel it in my soul that my life was about to change and I was so ready.

I had so much energy from dinner that I couldn't go to sleep so I hopped on my laptop and started looking for apartments. I emailed the potentials about rates before logging onto Facebook to see what my friends were up to. I finally grew tired of scrolling on the internet and opened my bible. I read a few verses of the third chapter of Ecclesiastes before praying and going to bed.

Everything was starting to work out for my good and I was so very happy about it. I couldn't wait to see what new heights I would reach working at Whitmore and Kramer. I was sure it would be a blessing.

Two

I woke up this morning feeling excited. It was finally my favorite day of the week, the day I get to go to church and give my worship to the Most High. I absolutely love going to church. Not only do I get to praise God, I get to fellowship with the people that I love and adore the most.

I said my morning prayer and a few breathing exercises before getting out of bed headed to the kitchen. I can hear my grandmother loudly singing along to one of Tamela Mann's songs. I could also smell the aroma eggs and sausage frying. I kissed my grandmother on the cheek and washed up to eat some breakfast.

My grandmother was in a rush to get out of the house, so I didn't ride with her to church today. It's the Women's Mission day program at our church, and since she's the president, she has to be there on time.

I decided to take my time getting ready this morning. I was feeling relaxed and just wanted to enjoy the moment of having the house to myself. After eating, I hopped in the shower and searched for something to wear. Since all of the women will be wearing either white or cream, I decided on a cream dress that I found at Ross's. It has long sleeves and stopped right below my knees. Once I put on the dress, I slid my feet into a pair of three inch black pumps, braided my hair into a goddess braid, put on a little lip gloss, grabbed my bible and headed to church.

When I arrived I, had to wait in the lobby since one of the women was praying. I wasn't the only who arrived late, so I quietly exchanged hugs with those waiting with me. The usher finally opened the doors to the sanctuary and we filed into the sacred room. As soon as I entered the sanctuary, I scanned the pews for my sister and smiled when I spotted her husband's bald head. I slid in to the empty space next to Hannah. I noticed how long her hair had grown so I ran my fingers through her hair and tugged at the hem of her purple dress.

"Good morning," I whispered, kissing my sister's cheek and grabbing my nephew from her lap. He smiled and immediately started playing with my necklace. His cute little dimples, light brown eyes and smooth brown skin make me want a baby of my own. When my niece, Leah, saw that I was there, she smiled and grabbed her coloring book so that she could sit next to me. She looked so cute in her pink dress and

23

ponytails. I kissed my niece's forehead and gave the deacon my attention.

Once praise and worship was over, the choir marched in and sang their hearts out. They had us all on our feet singing along and clapping our hands. We had alter prayer and listened as one of the women of the mission read a paper on restoration before the offering and then my favorite part: we heard the word. Pastor Simon taught us about living in the fullness of the Most High. I found myself nodding my head and jotting down notes as he delivered the message. I was loving the sermon, and apparently, so was half of the church. People were in different phases of worship evidenced by shouting, standing up and clapping. Some had tears falling from their faces, yelling out 'Hallelujah and 'Praise God' when pastor said something their souls could resonate with. The Most High definitely had a word for His people today.

I was definitely filled with the Holy Spirit by the time church was over. I couldn't wait to share what I learned with someone else. I was looking forward to applying what I learned today in my life.

The women's mission prepared dinner for everyone after service so we all headed over to the fellowship hall to eat. I noticed my grandmother in her all white suit and matching hat as soon as I walked in the room. She's tall and curvy with a mole above her lips on the right side of her face. My grandmother saved a table for us so that we could all sit together

"How's everyone doing today?" she asked once we were all seated.

"Blessed by that word pastor preached," Hannah said. "That was definitely what I needed."

"Right. I needed to hear that today, too," I added.

"Yes sir! Pastor was on fire today," my grandmother said.

"I didn't see him on fire grandma," Leah said.

"It's a figure of speech, baby. It means he did a really good job."

"Oh. Why didn't you just say that grandma?" Leah asked and we all laughed.

"Girl, hush and have a seat," Hannah said.

"Leave that child alone. She can ask grandma whatever she wants. Come here, baby." My grandmother sat Leah on her lap, hugged her and smiled.

The women working in the kitchen started passing out plates, and once we were served, we stuffed our faces with turkey, ham, macaroni and cheese, greens, dressing and yams. I was so full I had to take my German chocolate cake to go. The women did their thing in the kitchen and I was so glad I wouldn't have to cook. All I wanted to do was go home and lay down. And that's exactly what I did.

When I woke up from my nap, I checked my phone for any missed calls or text messages. I really don't know why since no one ever calls or texts with the exception my best friend, Miriam. And, of course, she did. When I replied back to her text, she told me she didn't make it to church today because she had to work. I told her she missed a great sermon and I'll share it with her the next day. Once I responded to Miriam's texts, I saw that it was a quarter after four and forced myself to get up. I didn't want to be up all night knowing I had to be at work in the morning.

I made my way into the living room to see what my grandmother was up to only to find her sitting at the table doing some scrapbooking. I smiled at her noting the peaceful look on her face. She is always doing some type of arts and craft and it is evident that it is relaxing for her. I guess the elementary school teacher in her will never die.

"Hey there, what 'ya doing?" I asked.

"Making a scrapbook for Sister Bishop. Her daughter is having another baby and she wanted to give her something unique."

"Looks good."

"Thanks. I see you were in there knocked out."

"Yes ma'am, I was. Sleep was so good I had to wake myself up. I don't want to be up late tonight."

"You sure don't. You'll have a hard time getting up in the morning."

"Exactly."

"So I guess it's safe to say that you like your job."

"I do. It's pretty demanding but I can handle it."

"God won't give you nothing too hard. If it gets hard, ask Him to give you the grace to get through it."

"Always."

"Mmm hmm." My grandmother held up her work. "What do you think?" she asked.

"It's really cute. I think she's going to love it."

"She better. I'm giving her some of my most creative ideas."

"You're funny."

"I'm serious."

"Trust me I know." Getting up from my seat, I told my grandmother, "I'm going to wash me some clothes. I'll see you later."

I went back to my room to prepare my clothes for the laundry and to catch up on one of my favorite TV shows: Empire. I know I shouldn't watch it, but it's so entertaining.

I did my laundry, got caught up on the last two episodes I'd missed, and read a few chapters of Terry McMillian's *Who Asked You?*. By the time I was done reading, I felt myself getting sleepy. I was out before I put my book down and turned the light off.

When I made it to work the next morning, I saw a woman that works in my building getting on the elevator with me. She had her eyes glued to her phone. She looked amazing! Her hair was short but it was in a really cute style. She had on a black and white checkered midi dress with a read belt and red pumps. Her make-up was flawless and she was wearing a beautiful handbag. I was in awe of her style. It wasn't until we were getting off of the elevator that she finally realized she wasn't alone.

"Good morning," she said.

"Good morning."

"You're new right?" she asked.

"Yes, I am. My name is Tamar."

"Nice to meet you, Tamar; I'm Sasha. I work on Oliver's team."

"Oh right. I've seen you in meetings, nice to finally meet you too."

"Yes, I've seen you, also. You work for Richard, right?"

"Yes, I do."

"Cool. Well, have a good day."

"You too."

Sasha strutted off towards her wing of the building with so much confidence. She was every bit of the word "diva." I needed some of her confidence to rub off on me.

I spoke to our receptionist and headed to my wing of the building. I sat my things down, turned my computer on and my eyes on the clock so that I could make Mr. Whitmore's coffee on time. While I waited until it was time to make the coffee, I printed out his agenda for the day and checked his calendar for any upcoming meetings. There were three meetings to attend today, a clear indicator that I have a very busy day ahead of me. I let out an audible sigh in anticipation of it all.

It was time for me to make Mr. Whitmore's coffee so I headed over to the kitchenette. I could hear laughter as I poured coffee grounds into a filter. I looked over my shoulder and saw two of the women from Mr. Whitmore's team looking in my direction. One of them was looking me up and down and smirking while the other laughed. The women shook their heads and walked away. I don't know what that was all about, but the same two women have been doing this ever since I started. I shook it off and made myself a cup of tea.

A few moments later Mr. Whitmore walked in. He said 'good morning' and headed to his office. I grabbed the folder with his agenda and messages and brought them to him. As always, he didn't say anything besides 'thank you,' which was my cue to leave.

When I returned to my desk, I was surprised to see Sasha was standing there since she has never come to my desk before. She actually looked kind of annoyed which confused me. I waited for her to speak.

"Did those two heffa's you work with say anything to you?" she asked.

"Who are you talking about?" I asked.

"Cynthia and Patricia."

"No, why?"

"Because they were making fun of your hair and clothes and I thought they might have said something to you."

"Wow. Um, no they didn't. Thank God."

"I can't stand office bullies. Let me know if they do. I'll have HR write them up. That's not cool."

"Thanks."

"You're welcome. I like your hair by the way. I wish I could wear mine's natural but I'm too lazy."

"Thanks. I love yours. I definitely can't pull off a short haircut."

"Thank you. Well, I'll let you get back to your day."

Sasha walked off with her confident stroll and I released a sigh. I thought about seeing Cynthia and Patricia giggling at me this morning and all of the other times. I guess they came back to get a good laugh, compelling me to look down at my outfit. I had on a powder blue button up shirt with black slacks and black flats. I didn't see anything wrong with what I had on; I was clean and I was matching. I touched my hair and felt the goddess braid that I wore the day before. *Women can be so mean and shallow*, I concluded, shaking my head.

Mr. Whitmore's first meeting was due to start in ten minutes so I headed over to the conference room. Cynthia and Patricia walked in, both suppressing smiles, so I decided to kill them with kindness. I spoke to both of the women and even complimented them on their outfits. They had the craziest look on their faces, but I smiled. They weren't expecting me to be nice to them since they were being so mean to me. I couldn't wait to tell my best friend, Miriam, about this.

I made it through the rest of my day by the grace of God. I was so glad to see the clock strike five o' clock I almost did the Nae Nae and I can't even dance. Yeah, I was so ready to go home.

I checked in with Mr. Whitmore to see if he needed me to do anything before I left, but thank God, he was already gone. I quickly shut down my computer, grabbed my purse and headed to the Bart station.

As I walked through the gates, I dialed Miriam's number hoping she wasn't at one of her jobs or on her way to school. I really needed to talk to my friend today; however, we have conflicting schedules so we're always missing each other. I smiled when I heard her voice on the other end.

"Miriam!"

"Tamar!"

"Oh my gosh! I'm so glad you answered. Can you talk?"

"Yeah, what's going on with you, girly?"

"I had a rough day at work today. I had the mean girl experience."

"Oh no! Really? What happened?"

"A couple of the women who dress to the gods laughed at my outfit, girl."

"Oh my gosh! Are you serious?"

"Yes, they hurt my little feelings."

"Aw, I bet. I'm sorry, boo. But um, I have to ask...what do you have on?"

"Just a blue button up shirt with some black slacks; nothing crazy. Mind you, these chicks were rocking BCBG dresses and Jessica Simpson pumps."

"Oh, so they're fly to deaf."

"You have no clue. They all look like they walk straight out of a department store every single day. Their make-up looks like they visit the Mac counter before they come in. Meanwhile, I stroll in rocking slacks from Ross and lip gloss from Wal-Mart."

She laughed, "Girl, you play too much."

"I'm serious," I joined her. "I feel so out of place, Miriam."

"Yeah, that sucks. Well, just remember, you're not there for your clothes, you're there for your brain. Keep doing your job. Your boss will notice your hard work, not your outfit."

"You're right. I don't know why that bothered me."

"Well I can understand why it bothered you. That's kind of rude to talk about someone's outfit in front of them."

"I didn't hear them say anything, but I saw them giggling. I guess they were talking about me in front of other people in the office because one of the ladies came and told me what was going on."

"That was nice of her."

"Yeah."

"Is she a glamazon, too?" Miriam asked.

"Yep, she's actually the prettiest one."

"I need to see these women."

"I'll sneak some pictures."

"Yes! Please do!"

"I miss you, girl. When are we going out for lunch or dinner? What's your schedule like?"

"I miss you too, girly. My schedule is crazy like those chicks at your job." We laughed. "I think I'll be free Thursday night. I have class and then I'm available. Want to do dinner?"

"Sure, let's do dinner."

"Cool beans. Well, let me get off this phone. I have to be at work in an hour and I want to finish some homework before I go. I love you, suga buga."

"Love you too, love bug."

I hung up with my best friend and felt so much better. I was two stops away from my station stop so I prepared myself to get off. I saw someone out of the corner of my eye waving at me and realized it was Sasha.

"Hey, girl, how was the rest of your day?" she asked.

"It was fine. How was yours?"

"Busy, of course. Did you run into those heffa's again?"

I laughed, "No, I didn't."

"Good. Well, maybe we can hang out for lunch some time. I'll tell you how to survive working for Richard. He's a special case."

"Oh wow. Yeah, that will be great."

"Good. Is this your stop, too?"

"Yep."

"I finally have a Bart buddy. All of the other women live in the other direction. I'm the only who comes to Oakland. What time do you go in?"

"Around 8:30 or so. I have to have Mr. Whitmore's messages and agenda ready when he comes in at nine."

"I see he hasn't changed. And please, call that fool by his first name when you're talking to me; we're not at work."

I laughed. "Okay."

"Well, I usually go to work around that time, too. Maybe I'll catch you in the morning. I get on the 7:55 train."

"Yep, me too."

"Cool! Well I'll see you in the morning."

Sasha walked away with her diva stroll and I smiled. I was glad I finally had someone to talk to. I'm not sure how long Sasha has been with the company, but I know she's been there long enough to give me the scoop. Tomorrow will be interesting.

Three

When my alarm clock went off, I fumbled around for my phone to hit the snooze button. I wanted to sleep in just a little bit longer. I wasn't ready to roll out of my bed, but reluctantly, I did.

I prayed, did my breathing exercises and stared at the ceiling. Ten minutes later I was pulling myself out of bed and dragging into the bathroom. I was thinking about what I had clean to wear and felt anxious. I decided today I'll put more effort into my outfit to prevent being the talk of the office. Being laughed at is not cool, especially as an adult.

I searched through my closet and thought I'd be like the other ladies and wear a dress. I never see the other women wear slacks. Maybe that's why they were laughing at me. I settled on a sleeveless black dress with a beige cardigan. I didn't own any heels like the other ladies wore, so I put on my three inch black pumps that I religiously wore to church. I put a little extra effort into my make-up as well. I put on some lipstick and some mascara and thought I looked cute.

I grabbed my things and headed to the Bart station. I noticed Sasha right away when I made it to the platform. She looked super cute in a hot pink midi dress. Her blazer and shoes were black and her purse was pink, black and cream. She looked amazing! I looked down at my own outfit and wanted to go back home and try again. If this was a competition, I definitely lost.

"Good morning, Sasha."

"Hey, good morning doll." Sasha looked at my outfit. "Look at you trying to step it up in the fashion department."

"Yes, trying."

"Well you put in some effort, that's all that matters. You look cute, though."

"I know you're just being nice, but thanks."

"Hey, a compliment is all a woman needs to be confident. Rock your outfit, doll."

"Thanks."

"So, has Richard said anything about the way you dress yet?" Sasha asked.

"No. Gosh, do I dress that badly?"

"No, he just likes his assistants to dress a certain way. I'm surprised he hasn't said anything to you about it yet."

"He hasn't said anything. And what way does he want his assistants to dress?"

"Sexy. Usually his assistants are the reason he gets accounts. You know men are visual creatures."

"Oh. Yeah, well, I didn't know that about him."

"Mmm hmm. See, what he does is have his assistants dress provocatively and flirt during meetings to distract the clients from what he's saying. His last assistant was really good at that. He got a lot of accounts because of her. He used to take her on shopping sprees all the time."

"Oh really?"

"Yep."

"What happened to her?"

"She ended up marrying one of their clients and moved to San Diego."

"Oh wow."

"Yep. She was that good."

"That's intimidating to hear."

"Don't be. Be yourself."

"That's easier said than done after hearing that."

"You'll be fine. Come on, our train is here."

I thought about what Sasha said about Mr. Whitmore and his expectations of the way I dress and I became so nervous. I'm not the type of woman who dresses sexy. That goes against my beliefs as a daughter of the Most High. I've been taught to dress modestly, to leave something to the imagination. The women at my job do the complete opposite. No one is walking around in freakum dresses or anything, but their outfits are so form fitting, they may as well. Wearing a blazer doesn't make it look professional, I don't care what any of them say.

We finally made it to work and went our separate ways. Sasha and I agreed to meet in the lobby at 12:30 for lunch. I was actually looking forward to it. I probably wouldn't have befriended Sasha on my own being that I'm intimidated by her beauty, but so far she seems to be cool.

I got right to work when I made it to my desk. For some reason I had a lot of emails and messages for Mr.

Whitmore. I checked his calendar and closed my eyes. We have four meetings to attend today. Great. I was just glad none of them would interrupt my lunch date with Sasha.

Mr. Whitmore finally walked in the office a little after nine. I quickly got up and followed behind him with his messages and agenda. He didn't seem like his usual, self so I made sure to be in and out of his office quickly. I didn't want to feel his wrath that I've overheard more times than I'd like.

"Wait," he said as I was walking out.

"Yes?"

"I'm meeting my wife for lunch today. Call that restaurant that she likes and make reservations, please."

"Will do."

I went back to my desk and set a reminder to call Crustacean's when they opened for the day. A few moments later I gathered myself together and headed to our first meeting of the day.

I was so glad that both morning meetings were short; I wasn't in the mood for all the big business talk. It was finally time for me to go to lunch and I was way past ready. I didn't have the energy to write up extra-long memos today. I had way too many emails to follow up on. I'll get to those when I returned from lunch. I grabbed my purse and headed to the lobby to meet Sasha. She was sitting on one of the benches scrolling through her phone laughing and shaking her head, when I caught up to her. When she saw me, she stood up and straightened her dress.

"Girl, these fools are too crazy on Instagram."

"Oh, yeah, I've heard."

"You heard? What, you don't have Instagram?"

"Nope."

"What about Snapchat?"

"Nope."

"Periscope?"

"Unt uh."

"Interesting. Well, what about Facebook?"

"Yeah, I'm guilty of having a Facebook page."

"Mmm hmm thought so. Everybody has at least one social media profile floating around." We laughed at that fact. "Okay what do you have a taste for?" she asked.

"I could go for some Chinese food."

"My kind of girl. Come on, I know a good spot around the corner."

Sasha and I walked two blocks from our office and ended up at some restaurant I've never heard of. The food smelled delicious and I couldn't wait to eat. We placed our orders after we sat in a booth.

"So how did you end up working for Richard?" Sasha asked.

"He found my resume on LinkedIn. I just graduated from San Francisco State University six weeks before I started working here."

"That's amazing. What was your major?"

"Marketing."

"Ha. Makes sense."

"What about you? How long have you been with the company?"

"Eight years too long. I need to move on so I can get a promotion, but I can't lie, I'm pretty comfortable. I make good money and I love the perks that come with working here."

"Yeah, I was way too happy when I got my first check."

"Trust me doll, I know."

"So were you friends with the last lady who worked for Richard?" I asked.

"I wouldn't say we were friends but I did know her. She was really beasty; all about making her money and Richard gave her a lot of bonuses. Like I said, she helped him close a lot of his deals, but not in a respectable way, if you catch my drift."

"Oh wow."

"Exactly. So be careful."

"You're scaring me."

"I'm sorry. I just want you to know what you're getting into, that's all. Richard isn't a regular boss. He sees green only. He's all about that dollar bill and will get it by any means necessary."

"That's interesting."

"You have no clue."

Sasha and I enjoyed our lunch and got to know a little more about each other. Sasha is from Oakland, graduated from San Jose State and has three sisters and two brothers. She's the only one of her siblings who doesn't have kids and she doesn't plan to. Along with telling me about her family life, she also mentioned that she loves fine men who make at least six figures. I listened in amazement. I have never befriended a woman who was so bold, so confident. She doesn't care what anyone thinks about her.

I didn't tell her much about me. My life is completely boring compared to the small dose she told me about her. I basically told her I grew up with my grandmother in Richmond, have one older sister, a best friend and no man. I kept my virginity and the relationship, or lack thereof, with my mother to myself. Talking about my life depresses me, especially the part about my mother.

When I made it back to the office I quickly replied to a few urgent emails and prepared myself for our next two meetings. Mr. Whitmore called me into his office a few minutes before it was time to head to the conference room.

"Come on in and have a seat, Tamar."

"What can I do for you, Mr. Whitmore?" I asked.

"You can call me Richard."

"Okay. What can I do for you, Richard?"

"I just wanted to fill you in on our next client for this afternoon."

"Okay."

"He's a really boisterous guy. He'll most likely say some things that will be sexist and misogynistic and I just want you to be prepared for that. Can you handle it?"

"Wow. Is that what's going to happen?" I asked.

"Yep, I'm pretty sure Mickey will say some things that are going to make you feel very, very uncomfortable."

"And you're okay with doing business with someone like that?"

"Yes, his personality doesn't pay the bills. His business does."

"I see."

"I've had people quit after encountering him more than once. He comes in quite often since he's one of my biggest clients. I just wanted to give you a heads up. Mickey is pretty hardcore."

"Thanks for the heads up. I think I can handle it."

"Great. Um, do one last thing for me."

"Yes?"

"Take off the sweater."

"Excuse me?"

"That sweater. Take it off. And I like the effort you've put in to wear a dress today; maybe you can wear something a little more fashionable next time, especially when we have meetings. It's easier for me to close deals when my assistants are easy on the eye."

"I'm not sure how to take what you said, Mr. Whitmore."

"Richard. And take it straight because that's how I gave it to you. Ask some of the other women here where to shop. Maybe they can give you a few pointers."

"Is that all, Richard?"

"Maybe a little red lipstick."

"I'll do my best to be pretty."

"You're halfway there. Come on let's head to the conference room."

I felt my body follow Richard, but my mind wasn't with me. My chest was heaving up and down, heart beating a mile a minute. I was trying to process the conversation we'd just had. I couldn't believe what he said to me. I don't know if his words or his tone bothered me the most, but I was definitely bothered. He was way too comfortable telling me to dress better. Sasha was right; I'm in way over my head. I really need to pray about this job. I wish I had time to pray right this second. My stomach was in knots and I couldn't focus.

Mickey Stuart was the rudest, most handsome man I'd ever met in my entire life. I did not like him at all. He had an intimidating personality, a loud mouth, the nicest smile and was extremely arrogant. Rightfully so I suppose. He owns a winery, a bed and breakfast in Napa and two restaurants in Marin and he's the most obnoxious man I've ever had to be around. He said every offensive statement about women that my ears have ever heard. In his eyes, we're only good for looking pretty and pleasing men in the bedroom. He let me know that my outfit wasn't sexy enough and even told Richard in front of me that he needs to take me shopping before the next meeting. He said if he has to look at a woman, the least she could do was turn him on. I felt so small. I was so glad when he finally left. I couldn't believe Richard let him talk to me like that. I couldn't wait to see Sasha after work to tell her about my afternoon.

When the clock struck five, I left my desk so quickly, I don't even know if I closed my computer down properly, and honestly, I didn't care. I just needed to get away from that place and fast.

The look on my face must have said how I felt because Sasha asked me what happened before I could tell her. I was so distraught I could barely form the right words to speak. I spoke so fast I didn't even understand myself.

"Richard made me mad. Mickey Stuart hurt my feelings. They both made me feel like the ugliest woman on the planet. I don't know if I can handle working here, Sasha."

"Oh no, doll, I'm so sorry. What happened?"

"Well after lunch Richard called me into his office to warn me about Mickey Stuart being a jerk and also to tell me to dress like the other women in the office. I couldn't believe it."

"I told you, girl. He's had a least four assistants before you came since Natalie quit six months ago. None of them could handle the job."

"It's not the job they couldn't handle, it's the requirements. I can handle the job just fine but hearing my boss tell me to dress better is kind of out of line. Oh and he told me to wear red lipstick. I don't know what I should do."

"I hate to say it, but either step it up in the fashion department, or find another job, doll."

"What?"

"Hey, I'm just saying. He's set in his ways and he means what he says."

"And what if I don't do what he asks?"

"He'll find a reason to fire you."

"What if I went to HR?"

"Girl, human resources won't do anything about it. They'll just get paid to keep their mouths shut."

"Are you serious?" I asked.

"Yep. One of Richard's assistant's tried to file a claim against him and they paid her to keep her mouth closed."

"Wow."

"Exactly. So if you can't handle having to dress differently to keep your job, you'd better start looking for another one."

"But I need my job."

"Well do what you have to do, doll."

I was so confused with the things I was hearing from Sasha, I could barely think straight. I had a lot of thinking and praying to do. This was not what I had in mind when I started this job. Just when I started to believe this job was a blessing, it's starting to feel more like a curse.

When I made it home, I called my sister to tell her about my day. I just couldn't believe the things I was told. This just couldn't be right. I needed my sister to tell me what I should do. It's easy for me to just quit, but it's so hard to find a job. I need some guidance.

"Hey, Hannah, what are you doing?" I asked, removing my shoes.

"Cooking dinner and trying to clean up this house. What's up with you?"

"Well, I had a really crazy day and I need your advice."

"What happened?"

"My boss told me that I need to dress better and to wear make-up. Red lipstick to be exact and one of his clients was so rude and so disrespectful to me that I'm ready to quit."

"Your boss did what?"

"Yeah."

"Can you say lawsuit?"

"Right, but I don't know if that's what I want to do, Hannah. I need to find another job fast."

"Do what you have to do, sweetie."

"I will, but in the meantime, what am I supposed to do?"

"Your job."

"Easier said than done, Hannah."

"Is it that bad?"

"Yes, it is. I had to sit in a meeting today with a man who told my boss in front of me that I wasn't attractive enough and that he needs to take me shopping."

"Oh my goodness! Are you serious?"

"I wish I wasn't."

"Aw love, I'm sorry."

"Me, too. I thought I finally found my dream job, but I guess not."

"Well, when your boss said he wants you to dress better, what exactly does he mean?"

"He wants me to dress sexy so that I can help him close deals."

"Wow, Tamar, what kind of company are you working for? You need to get out of there."

"Yeah, I know."

"I'll definitely be praying for you."

"Thanks. I'll let you get back to your life. I needed to vent. Kiss my niece and nephew for me. Love you guys."

"We love you, too. Keep me posted."

"Okay."

I hung up the phone with my sister and felt even more defeated. She didn't tell me anything useful. I guess I have to take this to God in prayer because no one I've told about my day has said anything that encouraged me.

I turned my phone off and got on my knees and prayed for discernment and guidance. I needed God to speak to me and to speak to me right now. I needed to hear a word from

Him because I was so confused about what was going on with me. I know that I need my, job but I don't know if I can handle this. Not under these circumstances.

After I prayed I logged into my bank account to check my balance. I stared at the amount that was deposited into my account last week and I couldn't even front; I was looking forward to seeing that amount deposited again in a few days.

I don't know. Maybe I can step my fashion up just enough to keep my job until I find another one. I can save up as much money as possible and pray that I'll make just as much at my new job that I am working for Richard.

Yeah, I'll do that. By the time Richard tells me that I'm not sexy enough, I'm sure God will bless me with another job. He has to. He said that He would provide for me and that the word He spoke over my life would not return to Him void. He said that He has plans to prosper me and I believe Him. So I'm counting on Him to do just that.

Four

Yesterday at work I told Sasha that I decided to step my fashion game up until I was able to find another job, so we decided to meet up to go shopping today. She was way too excited to help me with my makeover and I actually was excited to go shopping. I have to admit, I don't have swag, and I could go for a more modern look. Being fly doesn't come natural to me like it does to my sister and Sasha. I need some help in that department. I decided that I'll be classy not sexy, which is still a different look than what I currently rock. I definitely dress like a church girl who's never been anywhere other than school and church.

As I was headed out to meet Sasha at Sun Valley mall in Concord, I saw that my grandmother was preparing for her book club meeting. She and some of the other women from the church get together every Saturday morning to discuss spiritual and inspirational books. I sat and chatted with her before I left.

"Hey, grandma, what's up?"

"God and my book club."

"What book are you ladies reading?"

"Chasing Destiny by Bishop T.D. Jakes."

"Sounds good."

"It's really good. You can read it when I'm done."

"Okay."

"Where are you going?" she asked.

"To the mall; I need some more clothes for work."

"What's wrong with the clothes you have?"

"Nothing, I just want some new stuff."

"Oh okay. Make sure you keep it sanctified and professional. Gone and get your shop on. And don't go down there spending all of your money."

"That's the plan. I'm meeting one of my co-workers there so I'll see you later."

"Okay. Have a good day."

"You, too." I kissed my grandmother's cheek and headed to the mall. One day she'll stop telling me what to do. One day soon I hope.

When I got to the mall, I headed straight to Macy's. Sasha told me to meet her in the shoe department and she was already there when I arrived, trying on a pair of five inch pumps. She was so into the shoes that she didn't see me sit down.

"Hey, Sasha."

"Hey, doll, what's up?"

"Ready to get this over with."

"Um, you have the wrong attitude, my dear. It takes time to get fly. We are not going to be rushing today."

"Whatever you say."

"See, now that's what I like to hear." We laughed and Sasha said, "Let's start with shoes and work our way up. Here, these are cute." She passed me a pair of peep toed heels. "Try these on. Size eight, right?"

"Yep."

I slid my feet into the fancy shoes and felt myself tense up. I have never walked in any heels this pretty or this high. I was glad they had a platform. Hopefully this added feature will save me from falling flat on my face. I sat in the chair twisting my feet from side to side admiring the pretty shoes on my feet.

"So are you going to walk in them or keep looking at them?"

"I'm nervous."

"Get up, girl."

I laughed. "Okay, I am. Don't laugh at me I've never worn this kind of heels before."

"I'm not going to laugh at you, doll. I'm here to help you. So stop stalling and get up."

I hesitantly got up and started prancing around the store. I was shocked that I was so comfortable. I didn't stumble or break my ankles like I thought I would. I walked around a couple of times in front of the mirror to see how well I was doing. I could see Sasha smiling as I checked myself out in the mirror. I couldn't front, I was feeling myself.

"I see you, girl," Sasha said.

"I'm rocking them, right?"

"Yes, you are. Here, try these ones." Sasha passed me a pair of black snake skin pumps. As soon as I put them on, I smiled. I loved them! I pranced around in those for a while before trying on two more pairs of heels. I absolutely loved every pair of heels that touched my feet. If my grandmother saw me, she'd pass out, calling on the name of Jesus as she hit the ground. The shoes I picked were everything but sanctified. Oh well.

I got all four pairs of heels and we headed over to the women's department. I was so nervous. I haven't gone shopping in so long, I didn't know what the latest styles were. I decided to remind Sasha that I didn't want to change my style too drastically.

"Okay, so remember I don't want to look extra sexy, just classy. I don't want anything with cleavage or anything that will hug my hips. My grandmother will kill me if I walk out of her house with something that shows my curves."

"I can do classy. We'll make it a little sexy but we'll leave the cleavage out. You can be sexy without flossing the ta-ta's."

"Okay, well, let's do this."

Sasha is really good at picking nice clothes. Everything that she picked out for me was cute. I tried on dresses, cute tops, even cuter skirts. I had a week's worth of skirts and dresses, and two weeks' worth of shirts. I was glad I decided to meet Sasha at the mall. She made sure everything I bought was on sale or the clearance rack. I can go shopping with her anytime.

"Okay, so you're all set for next week. Richard is going to be surprised to see you come in the office looking all brand new."

"Yeah I just hope that he likes it. This money I spent was a part of my moving funds."

"Trust, he's going to like it. And you'll save up again. When are you trying to move?" Sasha asked.

"Soon and very soon. I'm ready to be on my own."

"Who do you live with?"

"My grandmother and I can't wait to move."

"Oh yeah, we're going to have to change that real soon. There is nothing sexy about living with someone if they're not you're man."

"Girl, I'm not worried about no man."

"You should be."

I laughed. "Whatever."

"I'm hungry. Let's get something to eat."

Sasha and I headed to Lucille's for a quick bite to eat. I was in the mood for some southern food and Lucille's never disappointed. We talked and laughed and had a great time. While I told Sasha a few more things about me, I didn't mention how involved I am in church mainly because I hadn't heard her mention it. I didn't want her to think I was the lame church girl, although I am. I actually hope some of her sassiness rubs off on me.

"Okay, so what are you going to do about your hair?" she asked.

"What's wrong with my hair?"

"I mean, nothing is wrong with it, but you know, that bun doesn't really say classy. It's more of an, 'I'm going to the gym real quick, hairstyle."

"Well tell me how you really feel."

"I'm just saying. If you're going to switch it up you may as well go all the way. I know someone who can hook you up. My girl does hair and she'll give you a discount since you're my girl, too."

"Thanks."

"Call her tomorrow. Maybe she can squeeze you in sometime this week. In the meantime I need you to go on YouTube and find some videos on how to make that mop on your head look fly. You can't be rocking a bun with those outfits we got today."

"You really know how to make a girl feel special."

"I know right!"

After Sasha and I fed our faces, we went our separate ways. I went home and looked at the clothes I bought. I smiled when I thought about how cute I was going to look. I tried on everything again, this time with the shoes. I really liked my new clothes. I looked more mature, like a grown woman. I appreciate that Sasha didn't pick anything out that made me feel uncomfortable. Nothing was too tight and nothing showed cleavage. I hope Richard likes my new look. I certainly do.

I took my new clothes off, hung them up in the closet and updated my resume. While I can admit that the new clothes boosted my confidence, I don't like that it was forced on me. I know that I needed to step my fashion game up, but I would have when I was ready. And to know that Richard wants me to look a certain way to please his clients still doesn't sit too well with me.

I submitted close to ten resumes to some pretty good companies. Hopefully I will hear back from someone sooner than later. I don't know how much longer I'll be able to pretend that I'm happy working for Richard because I'm definitely not.

======

I woke up the morning and was so glad that it was Sunday. My spirit was still heavy though. I would definitely be at church today and I'll definitely be going to the altar.

My grandmother was up, moving around in the kitchen when I went to the bathroom. I could hear Hezekiah Walker blaring from the speakers. I hummed along to Every Praise as I showered. I felt like I was moving slowly so I put a pep in my step so I could make it to church on time.

I was still excited about my new clothes and couldn't wait to see how I looked in them so I decided to wear one of my new dresses. I wanted to see how it would feel to look brand new for a change. Everyone is used to seeing me dressed rather low-key. It would be nice to see if anyone notices my more mature look. I put on my black midi dress with a red belt and black pumps. I did a double look in the mirror and smiled. I loved my new outfit. I finally looked like a 25 year-old woman.

Once I was dressed, I started removing the flexi rods that were in my hair. After I submitted resumes last night, I searched on YouTube for natural hairstyles I could try and found a video with some girl using flexi rods and conditioner. I started to smile as I played with the curls. I loved my hair. I took a selfie and sent it to Sasha. She replied back with compliments and smiley faces. I then applied my make-up, grabbed my bible, my purse and headed to McDonald's.

I stuffed my face with a sausage Mc Muffin and drove to church since I didn't have time to sit in the parking lot and eat. I don't like missing devotion at church and I wanted my regular seat. If I get there late, I'll have to sit by the people who talk throughout service. I'm not going to be able to do that. I need to hear what thus says the Lord.

Miriam was pulling in the parking lot as I was getting out of the car. I smiled and waved at my bestie. I haven't seen her since we had dinner a few weeks ago. I couldn't wait to see what she thought about my new look. As soon as she got out of the car we hugged.

"Hey, girly, look at you." Miriam tugged at one of my curls. "I barely recognized you. Where is my bestie?"

"You like?"

"Yes, it's really cute. You did this?" she asked.

"Yep, got it from YouTube."

"Is this a new dress?"

"Yep, cute, huh?"

"Yes, it is. I would have never imagined you wearing anything like it."

"Me either but I was ready to switch my swag up."

"Your swag, huh?"

"Yep."

"Oh okay, girly, I see you. Look at you being all modern."

"I know right."

"That job is turning you out already I see."

"Girl, you have no clue. I have to tell you about my boss. He's a trip."

"Ut oh, is he trying to hit on you?"

"No, crazy. That would probably be better, though."

"What? What's going on?"

"He wants me to change the way I dress to impress his clients."

"Say what?"

"Yeah."

"And what does he expect for you to wear?"

"He wants me to look sexy."

"Is that even legal for him to say that to you?"

"Not at all. The women I work with dress that way so he wants me to do the same."

"Oh wow. You need to let him know that you are saved and sanctified and you don't get down like that!"

We laughed and I said, "For real, though."

"We have to pray God moves you to a career that won't pressure you to dress like you're part of the world. That sounds crazy."

"Yeah, it is."

"Come on. We have a worship to give."

Miriam and I went inside the sanctuary and sat in our regular seats; fifth row from the pulpit. We've been sitting in this area since we were 12 years-old. I saw Hannah and the kids sitting with my grandmother. I smiled and blew kisses to my niece, who pretended to catch them. Hannah raised her eyebrows when she saw my hair and smirked. I shook my head and giggled.

Church was just what I needed. I prayed and cried and prayed some more. I asked God to reveal to me what I should do about my job. I hope I see His confirmation really soon. I also asked for peace while I wait for this storm to be over. I didn't see this situation getting any better any time soon, but I have faith God will see me through it.

After service, Miriam invited me over to her parents' house for dinner. Since I hadn't seen them in a while, I went along knowing her brother would be there. For as long as I could remember I've had a crush on Miriam's older brother, Ezra, and I can't wait to see those dimples. I'd never try to get with him or anything, but it doesn't hurt to be in his presence for a while.

"Ooo, look at you with your cute little dress and fancy hairstyle. Come here let me see you, girl." Miriam's mom, Mrs. Morris, ran her hands through my hair. "I like this hairstyle on you, girl. Miriam, you have to do this to my hair."

"I'll try it, Mom."

"I'm going to look good too, girl. Just like Tamar." We all shared a laugh.

"It does look nice on you," Ezra said.

"Thank you."

"Hey there, Tamar. Long time, no see. How's it going?" I looked up and saw Miriam's dad, Mr. Morris walking from the kitchen.

"Hey, Mr. Morris. It's going pretty good."

"What you been up to, sweetheart?"

"Just working, trying to find myself a place to move."

"How's the new job going?" Mr. Morris asked. He was a tall man with a big stomach and a deep voice. He looks so intimidating but he's so nice.

"I like my job but not my boss."

"Aw, that's too bad. That's normally how it goes. Either you like the job and not the boss or you like the boss and not the job. I'll be praying for you sweetie," Mrs. Morris said.

"Thanks I definitely need it."

"Are you going to try and find another job or stick it out?" Mr. Morris asked.

"I'm looking for another job."

"That bad, huh?"

"You have no clue."

"Well you should be able to find something with that fancy degree you have. Miriam should have gone to San Francisco State with you and she would be finished with school by now," Mrs. Morris said.

"Mom, please don't start that. I'm almost done with school. I have two more semesters to go."

"Good and you can be out of my bank account because you'll have your own money."

"Yes, praise God in advance!" Miriam started to stomp her feet.

"Ya'll are too much," I giggled and sipped my iced tea.

"You already know how we do over here." Mrs. Morris winked at me.

"If you want, I can give your resume to my boss," Ezra offered.

"She don't want to work with you," Miriam said.

"Don't be a hater."

"Whatever."

"What do you do again?" I asked Ezra.

"I'm in sales but it's a large company. I'm sure you can get in somewhere."

"Okay, yeah, give me your email address and I'll forward it to you."

"Bet."

I looked at Miriam and smiled. She rolled her eyes and shook her head. She knows I have it bad for her brother.

After I fed my face, Miriam and I went to her house for a little girl talk. I noticed my friend giving me the side eye during dinner when her mom asked me about my new look. I didn't take offense to it because I knew why she did it. She wasn't used to seeing me with new clothes and a new hairstyle. I knew she only asked me over because she wanted to grill me to death.

"So, what's up with this new look of yours?" she asked.

"Dang! Can I sit down first?"

"Sit down. Now, what's up this look?"

"Is it that bad?" I asked.

"It's not bad it's just not the Tamar I know."

"I'm just trying to keep my job, girl."

"And you think we serve a God that will allow you to be in lack because someone wants you to dress like a thot?"

"Um, no, but I don't want to lose my job right now. And I definitely don't look like a thot."

"Well, when do you want to lose it? It's not like you've been working there your whole life. You know how it is without the money."

"Yes, and I hated it," and we chuckled.

"I feel you but don't become a scripture statistic. You already know God doesn't want us to put money over integrity."

"Yeah, I know and I still have my integrity, Miriam. All I did was buy a new dress and put some curls in my hair. You act like I have on a freakum dress and a twenty inch weave."

"I mean, it's not that bad, but it's just not you."

"Well, thanks for your opinion."

"I'll definitely be praying for you. The spirit of Jezebel is certainly in there because you are not thinking like yourself anymore."

"That's kind of rude to say, don't you think?"

"It's the truth, though. Sorry if it's too harsh but it's real."

"Hmm." There was a very uncomfortable silence between me and my friend. "Well, okay. I'm going to get going so I can get ready for work. I'll talk to you later."

"I hope I didn't make you mad, Tamar."

"Not at all. Love you, talk to you later."

I hugged my best friend and went home. She did make me mad but I didn't want her to know. I'm already mad at myself. She's just confirming the little guilt that I have in my spirit. I really didn't need her to add her two scents.

When I made it home, I saw that I had two text messages from Hannah. She wanted me to call her when I had a chance. I rolled my eyes and let out a sigh. I already knew what she wanted. I know that she's calling because she has something to say about my hair and new dress. I can't with my sister right now. Miriam was enough.

I walked into my grandmother's house and saw that she was sitting on the couch watching Once Upon A Time and eating a slice of apple pie. She looked over her glasses at me as if she wanted to say something. I joined her in the living room.

"Who made the pie?" I asked.

"Sister Jones. And who made this woman I'm looking at?"

"What are you talking about?"

"You look like a brand new woman. Is this the outfit you bought yesterday?"

"Yep, you like it?"

"It's nice. It just doesn't seem like anything you would wear. Your co-worker picked it out, didn't she?"

"Yeah, she did."

"Mmm."

"Mmm what, grandma?"

"You look like your mama."

"That's not a compliment, you know."

"It's the truth."

"Okay, grandma."

"Be careful of the new friends you make. Don't let that devil lead you away from God."

"I won't. I'm about to get ready for work. Goodnight."

I went into my room, closed the door and sighed. I really wasn't in the mood for any of my grandma's bible lessons on life tonight. I didn't want to hear any of her anecdotes or Jesus' parables. Not tonight. And then she had the nerve to say that I look like my mom. Why would she say that to me? She knows how I feel about that lady. I knew people would have something to say about my new look, but I didn't think it would bother me so much. Can a sista live? Dang.

I didn't even bother texting or calling my sister back. The judgement and criticism from Miriam and my grandma was enough. I don't want to hear another word from anybody. I still can't believe my grandma said I look like Eve.

I bet that's why Hannah is calling me, to tell me I looked like our crazy mother today. Nope, I won't be calling her back tonight.

Anyway, I don't care what anyone has to say about me. I like my new look and I really hope that Richard likes it so I can keep my high salary paying job for a little while longer so I can move out of my grandmother's house. Then I will be able wear whatever I wanted. I know I shouldn't stay because of the money but there's no other reason I'm staying. God knows my heart so He understands why I'm doing what I'm doing.

Or does He?

Five

When I got to work this morning I was anxious for Richard to show up because I wanted to see his reaction to my new look. Today I was wearing a purple button up shirt with a black high-waist skirt and black snake skin pumps. I was definitely feeling myself in this outfit. I know I looked good because I even had a few men say 'good morning' to me on the Bart. That has never happened to since I've been working here, and I mean never. I was looking like a grown woman and it was being noticed. I can't front, I kind of liked the attention I was receiving. It felt good.

Richard finally came in and a smile instantly appeared on his face when he saw me. I had my curly hairstyle, painted lips and cute high heels popping. I was looking like a new woman and it appeared that my boss was satisfied with my new look.

"Well, hello, Tamar. How are you doing this morning?"

"I'm great, Richard. How are you?"

"Not bad at all." Richard looked me up and down with a smirk on his face. "You're looking very nice today."

"Thank you."

"Coffee?"

"It's brewing."

"Do me a favor? When it's ready, pour the cream and sugar in my coffee at my desk, okay?

"Sure. Okay."

Once the coffee was done brewing, I brought Richard's cup, cream and sugar on a platter and fixed it as he watched me. I felt his eyes going up and down my body as I stirred in his cream and sugar. I took a step back and made eye contact with him. The way that he stared at me gave me a feeling I've never felt from him before. I felt butterflies! I can't front, I liked the way he was looking at me. I silently asked God to forgive me for liking the lustful way my boss was staring at me. I'm tripping. I need to clear my head. I cleared my throat and asked, "Is that all, sir?"

"What's on my agenda?" he asked.

"It's in the folder as it's always been."

"Read it to me, please."

I tucked in my full lips to suppress a sigh and read Richard's agenda for the day. My lips quivered as I spoke. I could feel Richard as he watched me. My heart was beating so hard I thought he'd see it through my blouse. I read off the three meetings we had to attend and that he was leaving early to have dinner with his wife. Richard smirked, nodded his head, thanked me and told me that I could get my day started.

When I got to my desk, I let out a hard sigh and closed my eyes. I'm not sure switching up my style was a good idea after all. I can definitely see I've opened up a door I'm not quite ready to walk through.

I opened my agenda and began to prepare for our upcoming meeting. I cringed when I saw that it was a follow up meeting with Mickey Stuart. I was not in the mood to deal with this fool. I closed my eyes, said a quick prayer and gathered the documents Mickey needed to sign. I told myself that today I wasn't going to let that rude piece of a man ruin my day.

I went into the conference room and set up. As I was walking back to my desk, I saw Mickey in the lobby. He did a double-take when he saw it was me. I chuckled and shook my head.

"Well, well, well, look who we have here. Richard's mousy assistant. I see that you can look like a grown woman instead of a girl fresh out of college. Looking good my dear."

"Good morning to you too, Mr. Stuart. How are you?"

"Better since I'm looking at a grown woman today. You know, I'm not really into little girls."

"That's a relief." Mickey raised his eyebrows and chuckled. "Excuse me, I need to get ready for our meeting. Can I show you to the conference room? Or can you be a big boy and make it there on your own?"

"I like this new attitude you got. Did it come with the clothes and new hairstyle?"

"As a matter of fact, it did."

"I like it, keep it up."

Mickey winked at me, adjusted his suit and went to the conference room. I rolled my eyes, shook my head and went to my desk. I thought about what I said to him and giggled to myself. I was shocked that I said the things that I did, but he brought out a side of me that I didn't know was in there. Maybe the new look gave me a new attitude as well. Or I could charge my snappy comebacks to being around Sasha. That girl has a mouth on her.

The meeting with Mickey went much better than last week. Surprisingly Mickey wasn't talking as rudely to me as he had previously. He was actually flirting with me throughout the entire meeting. He kept asking me to pour his water. Instead of sliding his paperwork across the table to Richard like he did in the last meeting, he'd ask me to hand it to him. The look on his face said he was happy to see me walking around the conference room.

I would be lying if I said I didn't like the way he was looking at me. I never, and I do mean never, had men look at me twice. Even if it was with lust in their eyes, it made me feel desirable and attractive, like a woman. I could only imagine how women like Sasha felt being around men like Mickey before today. Now I understood. And that's not good.

The rest of the day went by pretty smoothly for me. Richard left early, and although he said that I could leave early, I stayed until my regular time to avoid having extra work to do the next day.

Sasha was waiting for me in the lobby once the work day was over. She looked fly in her all black romper and hot pink pumps. I hadn't seen her all day because she had an offsite meeting. We had some catching up to do.

"Well, hey there, doll."

"Hello to you, too. How are you? I haven't seen you all day."

"It was crazy busy, girl. I closed a deal, got a new client, and bagged a cutie after my meeting. Yeah, it was a great day for me." We laughed. "How was yours? Did Richard like your outfit?" she asked.

"My day was great and yes he did. Mickey Stuart came by today and I surprised myself by being a smart butt towards him."

"Did you? Ooo wee! Must be the new clothes."

"Omg Mickey said the same thing." We laughed some more.

"Oh, I can definitely hear him say something like that. He is a mess."

"Yeah, he is."

"Well I'm glad you had a good day in your new outfit."

"It felt like the first day of school."

"Right! Felt real brand new, huh?"

"I sure did and it felt so good."

"I'm glad your day was great. Keep it up so you can get one of those infamous bonuses Richard is known for giving and treat me to a fancy dinner."

"I'll do my best."

The rest of the week went great. Richard complimented me all week long on my outfits and our meetings were much more relaxed. Everything was great. I was actually looking forward to going to work, something that I hadn't felt in a couple of weeks.

I went shopping over the weekend and was anxious to get to work that Monday. I arrived to work a little earlier than usually because I wanted to see what Richard's reaction would be to the outfit I was wearing. Yes, the compliments are starting to go to this big head of mine.

Today I had on a beige midi dress with beige peep toe pumps and a black blazer. I looked so fly I had to take a selfie and post it on Facebook, something I never do, but I was feeling myself.

When I arrived at the office, I checked my email for anything urgent and printed out Richard's itinerary for the day. Just as I was placing the papers inside of a folder, Richard strolled in looking nice and dapper as usual.

"Good morning, Richard. How are you today?"

"I'm pretty good, Tamar. How's my day looking?"

"Busy, of course. Here." I gave him the folder. "I'll bring your coffee in a sec."

"Thanks."

Richard made a few moans and groans as he went over his paperwork. I placed his coffee cup on his desk so that I could add his cream and sugar. I felt Richard watching me as I stirred his coffee. I did my best not to blush, but I'm not sure if I was successful or not. I actually liked that he watched me. I know, I know. He's married and I'm a child of God, but I'm also human. I like that he sees me as a woman and not a church girl.

"You look nice today."

"Thank you."

"Smell nice, too. What are you doing for lunch today?"

"Probably going somewhere with Sasha."

"Cancel that, you're going out with your boss today."

"I'd like that."

"Good, pick a nice spot and make us some reservations."

"Will do."

I went back to my desk and squealed! I don't know why, but I was excited to be away from the office with Richard. I couldn't wait to see why he wanted to take me to lunch. Hopefully it's about this infamous bonus I've heard so much about. If so, I'll be looking for apartments this weekend.

My day went by pretty quickly and I was relieved about that. Richard had two meetings that we attended, which took up half of the morning. I had a lot of notes to translate and I was typing up a memo when Sasha strutted over to my desk. I heard her fancy heels click-clacking on the marble floor before I saw her face.

"Hey, doll, how's it going?"

"Busy. What are you up to?"

"Just finished up a conference call, now I'm ready to feed my face. You hungry?"

"Yeah but I'm going to lunch with Richard."

"With Richard? Really?"

"Yeah."

"Did he invite you?"

"I didn't invite myself, Sasha."

"Well this is good news. Ooo! Maybe you're getting a bonus. Hey!"

"I sure hope so. More money never hurts."

"Right. Well, okay, I'm going to find someone to treat me to lunch. I'll talk to you later." Sasha winked at me before strutting back to her side of the building. I shook my head. That woman is too funny.

"Are you ready?" I turned to see Richard leaning up against the door frame.

"Um, yes. Let me send this email and send for your car, then we can go."

"Yes ma'am."

Richard went back into his office for his wallet. I quickly sent the email, called Richard's driver, touched up my lipstick and grabbed my purse.

The driver had Richard's car waiting when we got out of the elevator. He opened the door for us and drove to the restaurant. Richard was quiet as he checked and sent emails from his phone. Me, I was anxious. I was so nervous. I didn't know what he wanted and he gave no clues as to what it was.

Once we reached the restaurant, Richard gave me his undivided attention. The waiter brought us glasses water, bread and menus before leaving the table.

"So, Tamar, how do you like working for me?" Richard asked.

"I like it. You keep me busy."

"Good, I like to hear that. I also like that you have stepped your wardrobe game up."

"Thanks I guess."

"Yep. So listen, I invited you to lunch to keep you posted. The next few weeks are going to be busy. I'll need you to be on point."

"Oh. Okay. What do you need me to do?"

"Soon I'll be meeting with some very important people and I'll need you to keep up this new look you've been rocking. The men I'll be meeting with are very big on being around beautiful, well-spoken women. And the more attractive you look and the sweeter you are, the easier it is for me to close deals."

"I see." I looked down at my plate and bit the inside of my jaw. Disappointment was painted all over my face.

"What? You seem disappointed."

"I mean, I am. This isn't what I expected when you hired me or asked me to lunch."

"What did you expect?" he asked.

"I don't know. I guess I expected my boss to be professional, respectful, and honest."

"So, you're saying that I'm not any of those things?"

"I mean, yeah, but in an abrasive kind of way."

"Is that so bad, Tamar?"

"Actually, yes, it is."

"You know you like my style. Don't front."

"Excuse me?"

"You heard me." Richard looked at me with a smirk and took a sip of his water.

"I don't know what you're thinking, but you have the wrong thing on your mind. Your arrogant attitude is not cute."

"Most women who are around me think it's cute. So back to business…like I said, keep up this look you have going. Mickey really liked it. Since this is our busy season, I'll be having a lot of meetings trying to get a lot of new clients and your attire will help me out a lot."

"Oh really?"

"Yes, I'll even fund your shopping spree. You can think of it as having a uniform."

"A uniform?"

"Yes, instead of wearing khaki's and a collared shirt, you'll wear beautiful dresses and nice heels. What woman doesn't want to wear that and for free?"

"I guess most women do."

"What, you're not most women?"

"No, I'm not."

"We'll see about that."

After lunch we headed back to the office and I finished up my day. I could barely think straight; my thoughts were all over the place. I was still thinking about the conversation I had with Richard at lunch. I couldn't believe my boss gave me his credit card so that I could go shopping for sexy work clothes. I've never heard of this happening before. While I know I should be offended by his gesture, I was actually flattered. What is wrong with me?

Miriam and my grandmother were right: this job is turning me into someone I don't recognize. And I'm starting to get scared of who I'm becoming because I like her.

Five o'clock finally came and I was way past ready to go. I shut down my computer, gathered my things and met

Sasha in the lobby. We walked to the Bart station for our evening commute. I waited until we were sitting down before I told Sasha about lunch with Richard.

"So, lunch with Richard was very interesting. He gave me one of his credit cards and told me to go shopping for more outfits like this. He's going to be having some important meetings with some men who likes pretty women and he wants me to be dressed to impress them."

"What! I am so jealous! Okay, I have to go with you. Girl, we're about to go to the best stores and spend all that man's money."

"Sasha, did you just hear what I said?"

"Yes, Richard gave you his credit card to go shopping with. What's wrong?"

"Nothing like this has ever happened to me. I'm flattered but I feel wrong for taking his credit card. What will his wife think?"

"You're not taking it. He gave it to you. And who cares what she thinks?"

"I do. This is wrong, isn't it?"

"Says who?"

"Says me. I feel bad."

"Why? It's not like you asked him, he offered."

"Yeah but he made me feel like I was in Pretty Woman or something. He made me feel cheap."

"Well, you know how he is, Tamar. I already told you what he's about and so did he in so many words."

"I know, it's just different to actually experience it. Has this ever happened to you?" I asked.

"Yes, it happens all of the time."

"Men give you money just because of the way you look?"

"Yes. Money, shoes, bags, take me places. All kinds of things."

"And you're okay with men doing these things for you just because you're pretty?"

"Yeah. Girl, what planet did you come from?"

"Whatever. I mean, I've seen movies but never experienced anything like this. I can't believe men really do stuff like that."

"Well, they do. Rich ones anyway. So let me know when you want to spend Richard's money so I can make sure you spend it right."

Our Bart train came and we hopped on. Sasha got a call and entertained whoever it was on the other line. Meanwhile I thought about the things Sasha said to me. I was raised so much better than to allow a man to talk to me the way Richard did, but why am I not running in the other direction? Why do I like the fact that some man has basically given me his credit card for a shopping spree? I've never been that type of woman. Why am I turning into that woman now?

Eve was that type of woman. Probably still is. I haven't seen her since I was eleven so I really don't know. Now I know why my grandma said I look like my mother. It's because she was always dressed to the nines, had her hair in this big curly hairstyle and always kept her make-up flawless.

I know that's why my grandmother never let me and Hannah wear flashy clothes or hairstyles when we were growing up. She was always on me about the clothes that I wear the most. I'm sure it's because I'm the spitting image of her daughter who left her to raise her kids while she ran the streets of Oakland. The way that Eve dressed led her to the reason why she isn't here with us. I'm convinced craving a man's attention is genetic because I'm starting to act like my mom, I mean, Eve.

Despite my boss making me feel like Julia Roberts, the rest of the week went great. Sasha and I went shopping and Richard was pleased with the new outfits that I bought. I thought he would say something about how much I spent but he didn't even budge. He even told me that whenever I needed more clothes to let him know and he'll give me his card again. I'm not sure how I felt about that. I knew that I shouldn't allow a married man to buy me clothes but I did. I felt kind of bad but not bad enough to decline the offer.

Richard closed two new deals this week so he decided to take his team out to dinner. Since Sasha doesn't work on Richard's team, and I didn't want to go alone, I asked Richard if she could come and he didn't hesitate telling me 'yes.' His eyes said he was happy she'd be there. I shook my head at his reaction and called Sasha to tell her the news. She agreed to meet me at the restaurant once she was done with her offsite meeting.

Richard offered to give me a ride since we're eating here in the city. I really don't want to be alone with Richard. I could have easily made up an excuse as to why I wouldn't be able to make it to the dinner to avoid my boss. However, my carnal mind wanted to see how my co-workers behaved outside of the office.

Once I closed the office down, I called for Richard's driver to pick us up and take us to the restaurant while everyone else went ahead of us. It was just Richard and I. I fumbled around in my purse to avoid making eye contact, but I could feel Richard staring at me. He finally spoke after what seemed like forever.

"You did an exceptional job the past couple of weeks, Tamar. I want to thank you for being so flexible. It was because of you that I was able to close my deals. You gave the eye candy my clients are used to seeing when they come here. I'm surprised that you're as charming as you are since you try to pretend that you're not, but I like it."

"I have to admit I wasn't really comfortable with you telling me to change the way that I dress but I'm glad that I did because I feel more confident in my skin."

"I knew that you would. I've been doing this for a long time. I know what my assistant's need in order to be successful."

"Interesting."

"It's true. Like you, all you need is the look, confidence and vernacular. Now that you've gotten the look and the confidence, you're almost there."

"And where is this place you think I should be?" I asked.

"The place of success, baby girl. Isn't that what you want out of life? To be successful?"

"Yeah but I don't want to have to compromise my faith or integrity in order to be successful."

"Compromise is a part of success, my dear. No one has made it to success without it. I'm not saying that you have to completely change who you are, but you will definitely have to do some things and make some decisions that will compromise what you believe life is all about." Richard ran his hand lightly over my chin. Why I liked it was beyond me but I did.

"I don't know. I don't think it has to be that way."

"If you find another way, my dear, let me know."

Richard and I locked eyes. He smirked and I cleared nothing from my throat. I felt like he was challenging me. His gaze was so intense, it was like he could see right through me. I swallowed and prepared to say something, anything. Before I could respond, we were at the restaurant.

I left the conversation I had with my boss in the backseat and put my professional smile on. I didn't want my colleagues to be able to see that I was rather flustered. Or was I intrigued? I honestly don't know what just happened between my arrogant boss and me, but I think I liked it. Oh gosh, that's not good. Not good at all.

Sasha was already at the restaurant when we arrived and I felt so relieved. I needed her strength because I was definitely feeling weak. I shook my head and smiled when I saw her talking to one of the marketing managers. Well, it was more like flirting. She had her head tilted to the side as she spoke and every now and then she'd play with his tie. He was smiling so hard I know the corners of his mouth hurt. It was fun to watch her make a grown man blush. I could never do anything like that since I'm not as bold or as confident as she is.

I watched her for a little while longer before one of the brand managers came over to me with a glass of wine. I gave Ralph the side eye and waved away the wine.

"Don't tell me that you don't drink," he said.

"What other way can I say that I don't partake in wine?"

"You're like a saint, you know that?"

"Yes, I do and now so do you."

"Wait, I was joking, but are you serious? You're one of those bible toting church girls?" he asked.

"I sure am." Ralph and I have gotten pretty close over the last few months. He and I have had many great laughs in between meetings but he also doesn't know who I truly am. I kept the fact that I'm an avid church-goer to myself. Now, I don't care who knows.

"Interesting. I'm surprised you work here."

"What does that mean?"

"Oh nothing. So how is it working for a guy like Richard? You know, being a church girl and all."

"And what exactly does that mean?"

"You know, a man who only hires beautiful and sensual women to help him close his business deals. What's your superpower?"

"My superpower?" I asked.

"Yeah, what is it that you do really well that will get his clients to sign a contract?" he asked, raising his eyebrows.

"I don't have one, Ralph."

"Well you'd better get one if you want to be here long-term."

"What are you saying?"

"If you don't help Richard close our deals, you won't last very long here."

"Really?"

"Yep. His last assistant was here for a month or so and he didn't get any new clients because his clients didn't find her very attractive so he fired her."

"Oh wow."

"My bad, I thought that you knew."

"I guess I do now."

"On that note, I'm going back to the bar. I'll see you Monday."

Ralph drank the glass of wine he'd brought over for me and got himself another glass. I shook my head and watched him guzzle down another drink before I scanned the room for Richard. I don't know why but I did. I shook off the thoughts I had about my boss and searched the room for my friend instead. Sasha finally parted ways with John and was now talking to the receptionist. I waved at her to get her attention. She grabbed a glass of champagne and made her way over to my table.

"Hey, doll, what's up?" she asked.

"Not much, just wondering why you didn't tell me that the last woman who had my position was fired because Richard thought she was ugly."

"I thought I told you that."

"No, you didn't."

"Oh. Well, how did you find out?"

"Ralph came over here acting like a drunk Kermit the frog and spilled the tea."

"He did?" She chuckled. "That's funny."

"Yeah, I guess."

"Why do you sound mad, doll?"

"I don't know. I guess I'm disappointed. I thought Richard hired me because he thought I was smart, not because he thinks I'm attractive."

"Who cares? You have a job that pays you well. That's all that matters."

"Is it?" I asked.

"Uh, yes, Tamar, it is."

"I don't know, Sasha. I don't feel the same way. I don't know if I can keep working for him."

"So, what are you going to do? Quit?"

"I don't know what I'm going to do yet."

"I'll tell you exactly what you're going to do. Keep dressing fly, being sassy and getting these checks. If Richard wanted to fire you, he would have by now. He obviously sees your potential which is why he told you to step your game up so he doesn't have to fire you. You're in the real world now. College is over. You have to grow up, Tamar."

"Wait a minute, are you siding with him?"

"Yeah, I am."

"Wow."

"Look, it's nothing wrong with a man wanting to have a pretty woman working for him. I know that's why I got hired and why I've been here for so long."

"So you're okay with being office eye candy?"

"I sure am. If that's how I get my check, than guess who's coming to the office looking like a lollipop every day? That would be me."

"I just never heard of anything like this happening before. This is new to me."

"Well, get with it. Just because you never heard of it doesn't mean it hasn't been happening. It's nothing new under the sun, doll."

"I guess."

"Have a drink and relax."

"I don't drink."

"You mean like, at work, or ever?"

"Ever."

"Are you serious?"

"Yes, I am. I've never drank liquor before."

"You've never had a drink?"

"Never."

"Like ever?"

"Never, Sasha."

"No wonder you're so uptight. We're about to change that, doll."

"I'm not having a drink."

"Yes, you are. There's a first time for everything and tonight you're about to have your first drink."

"I don't want to."

"Yes, you do."

"What? Sasha, no, I don't."

"Just a sip."

"Okay, one sip and that's it."

"That a girl!"

I let her get me a glass of champagne. I didn't think about what I was about to do, I just did it. I wasn't in the mood to think anymore. I said I wanted Sasha to rub off on me and now she has.

I sipped the bubbly drink and smiled. I can't believe I actually drank for the first time. I guess a small part of me wanted to try it. And to my own surprise, I actually liked it a lot. I felt nice, so nice that I had myself another glass. I felt free. I was laughing and giggling, having a very good time. I didn't feel as guilty for having a drink as I thought I would. I mean, it's just a little champagne. It's not like I'm going to get hooked, right?

Six

"Excuse me can we get another glass of white wine please? Thanks." The waitress took our order and left. I looked over the menu for another appetizer while I waited for the waitress to bring Sasha and me another glass of wine.

"Look at you. You're just a little lush wine connoisseur now aren't you?"

I laughed and said, "Yep and it's your fault."

Sasha dramatically placed her hand on her chest. "Mine?"

"Yes, yours. You're the one who gave me my first glass of wine. I've been hooked ever since."

"Um, I gave you your first glass, not a bottle. You got hooked on your own, doll. Take some responsibility for your own lush actions."

"Oh whatever," I verbally pushed her words away Are you going to have another appetizer with me?"

"Yep, get some potato skins this time."

The waitress came back with our wine and took our orders. I almost ordered another glass of wine but remembered I had to drive. I still needed to go to Target anyway. I needed some cleaning supplies for my new condo.

"So what are you doing after we leave here? It's Friday night and I know you're doing something naughty," I said.

"You already know. I'm hooking up with Kamal." Sasha made a naughty face.

"Must be nice. I'm jealous."

"You shouldn't be. Go ahead and invite a cutie pie over to help you break your new place in."

"That is not even my style."

"The way you're guzzling that wine down I can't tell."

"Shut up," I giggled. "I need to clean up tonight since I won't have time the rest of the weekend. It's my nephew's first birthday party so I'll be at my sister's house all day tomorrow."

"Sounds fun," Sasha said sarcastically.

"You're such a meanie."

"So!" We laughed again. "Have your sister seen your new place yet?" she asked.

"Yep, she said 'congratulations' with her lips, but was judging with her eyes."

"Well, don't let that get to you. You've earned that beautiful place. You worked hard, saved all of your money, so you deserve it. You need to have a party in that thing."

"A party? And who would I invite?"

"I don't know. Your friends, a couple of cutie pies."

"Sasha, I don't know any cutie pies."

"Leave that part to me."

"Oh gosh."

"Stop being a lame. Pick a date and it's on."

"I'll think about it."

After we left BJ's I went to Target. I took my time strolling through the aisles putting things in my basket that were not on my list. This always happens when I come to Target. I was standing in the aisle with the air freshener's when my phone rang. It was Miriam.

"Hey, girl, what's up?" I asked.

"Not much, how are you? What are you up to?"

"I'm good, at Target getting a few things. What are you up to?"

"Just getting home. I saw your grandmother earlier and she told me that you moved. Why didn't you call and let me know? You haven't invited me over to see your new spot or nothing."

"I'm sorry, girl. I've been so busy with work and getting settled. I wanted to wait until I got my place together first, you know."

"No, actually I don't know. What's been up with you, Tamar?"

"What do you mean?"

"Your grandmother told me she hasn't spoken to you since you moved out. I haven't seen you at church. Is everything okay with you?"

"Yeah, I'm good. I'm fine. Work is just busy, that's all."

"Is your boss still treating you like a piece of meat?" she asked.

"He's better now."

"I wonder why."

"And what does that mean?"

"I've seen the pictures you've posted on Facebook lately. I see you changed the way you wear your hair. You have a sew-in weave, right?"

"Yeah and?"

"And that's not like you."

"Well now it is."

"Yeah okay. And who is that woman you were in the picture with?"

"That's my girl, Sasha."

"Your girl, huh?"

"Yeah."

"Why haven't you introduced us? I thought we were girls, too."

"I don't know, Miriam. I just haven't."

"Am I not good enough to meet your new friends?"

"Really, Miriam?"

"Yes, really."

"You're tripping. I'm about to pay for my stuff. I'll call you later."

"Yeah okay, Tamar."

I hung up the phone with Miriam and felt annoyed. I didn't like the fact that my grandmother is telling my business or that someone I've known all my life is questioning what I'm doing with my life. This is exactly why I've been keeping to myself.

Once I left Target I headed home. Home as in the place where I pay rent and live alone. It felt so good to go home to my own place and not to my grandmother's house. I've been in my condo for a month now and I love living like a grown woman.

My grandmother was surprised that I moved out, and because of that decision, my relationship with my grandmother has become strained. Even my sister and I have had a rift in our relationship. Ever since I started working for Richard and became friends with Sasha, things between my sister, Miriam, and my grandmother have changed and I honestly don't know why.

They're not feeling my new look or that I moved out without giving what my grandmother felt was ample notice. Okay, fine, I was wrong, but really? It's not like I snuck and moved out so I really don't understand why she's so upset. I told her as soon as I was approved. I didn't know they'd let me move in three weeks later. Whatever, I'm not going to overanalyze my grandmother's attitude.

I sat my bags down and took my heels off as soon as I made it inside. I crashed on my couch and rubbed my feet against the carpet and thought about work, thought about my grandmother, thought about the conversation I just had with Miriam. It always seems like when one or two areas of your life are going good, another area is starting to fall apart. Things have been going really, really well at work. I can see that our clients are more respectful to me now that I've switched up my style, and we've been closing a lot more deals.

Before I switched up my style the clients would ignore me during meetings, but now they address me by name.

Richard gave me a bonus because, according to him, I'm the reason his new clients have been closing the deals. I'll be making sure he closes more deals because I love the bonuses and shopping sprees. The bonus from Richard is how I moved into my condo.

Moving into my own place has been bittersweet. I'm loving that I have my own place and that I am finally providing for myself. However, the fact that I haven't spoken to my grandmother since I moved out kind of makes it a bitter moment. Her attitude instantly changed when I told her I was moving out. Since I knew she wasn't happy for me I've been keeping my distance. Maybe I'm wrong, maybe I'm not. I don't know. The phone works both ways, she can reach out to me, too. She's clearly still upset that I left and is being rather immature about the situation. Whatever. And Miriam has her nerve calling me trying to go in on me. She needs to mind her own business and finish school instead of worrying about what I'm doing. I don't have the energy to deal with all of that anyway. I'm trying to keep my own life together.

My nephew's first birthday party is tomorrow and I'm so excited to see his reaction to everyone singing happy birthday to him. I'm also excited to see my family. I haven't been to church in a while so I haven't seen anyone. My grandmother will also be there and hopefully she's not mad anymore so we can move forward. I really haven't seen my sister either. I've been busy working and trying to get my condo together. Since this is my first time living on my own I had to start from scratch with everything and I've been having a ball decorating.

I was still a little tipsy from the two glasses of wine I had earlier and was starting to get sleepy so I quickly wrapped my nephew's gifts and climbed into bed. I decided I would get up early and clean my condo. That would not be happening tonight.

When I woke up in the morning, I had a slight headache. I'd forgot to take some aspirin before going to bed. I've learned the hard way that if you drink too much, you sometimes wake up with a headache. I stumbled into my bathroom, took two aspirins, and lay back down. I woke up two hours later feeling a lot better. I looked at the time and jumped up to get dressed. I told Hannah I'd help her set up. I was supposed to be at her house at noon, and it was 11:10.

I hopped in the shower, threw on a sun dress, grabbed my nephew's gifts and headed out to my sister's house. I was so glad I was going against traffic so it didn't take much time to get to Hercules from Emeryville. Bay Area traffic is a beast, even on the weekend.

When I got to Hannah's house, some guy was in her backyard blowing up the jumper. Leah was running around the house and Mark was sitting on the couch holding Mark Jr. Hannah was walking around giving orders to her friends who were already there helping out and trying to put together the party bags. I put my things down and took over the party bags for my sister. She smiled at me, said 'thank you,' sighed and went to pay the guy who was setting up the jumper. Leah finally noticed me and joined me in the kitchen.

"Hi Aunty Tam Tam. You look so pretty. I like your dress. And your hair. It's curly this time."

"Hi, Leah. Yes, my hair is curly this time. Thank you, baby, but you look prettier."

"Thank you! Aunty it's little Mark's birthday party. I'm gonna have fun. I'm gonna jump in the jumper all day long until that man comes back and pick it up."

"Is that right, baby?"

"Yep. You gonna jump with me aunty?" she asked.

"I sure will baby. We have to do it after everyone else leaves so I don't crush the other kids."

"Yeah, you gotta wait because you will crush them with your butt because it's big, aunty."

I suppressed my laugh. "Girl, go play."

Leah skipped out of the kitchen into the backyard. All of the adults who overheard my niece laughed. I shook my head and continued stuffing the party bags. Hannah finally came back inside with Mark, Jr. on her hip checking on everyone's progress. She looked me up and down with a smirk, made a sound that said, "You think you're cute," and checked on the spaghetti she was cooking. I bit my bottom lip and put my head down. I knew she would have something to say when she saw my outfit and my hair. I've been going to the hairstylist Sasha recommended for a while now and have been getting a weave sown in. Today I was wearing a long, curly weave, and my sister isn't used to me wearing my hair like this. I know that's why she made that noise. She'll adjust, just like I did. Besides, I *do* look cute.

Before I knew it, Hannah's house was filled with people lounging and kids running around. Music was playing, food was being served and the kids were having a good time. Of course, little Mark fell asleep during the party. Leah kept her word and stayed in the jumper the entire party. It was a really good turnout. I saw family members I hadn't seen in a while. I even had a chance to see my grandmother, which was very awkward. She took one look at me and gave me her look of disapproval. She didn't talk to me much. That actually hurt my feelings.

After the party was over and everyone left, I kept my own word and hopped in the jumper with Leah. The rental guy finally came to pick up the jumper and Leah reluctantly got out. She was out of the jumper all of twenty minutes before she fell asleep on the couch. I kissed her forehead and carried her into her room.

By the time I came back into the living room, Hannah had put Mark, Jr to bed and her husband was in the den watching ESPN. I helped my sister clean up and pack up the leftover food.

"Nice turnout," I said, putting a lid on some fruit.

"Yes, it really was. Thanks for all of your help."

"Of course."

"Make sure you take some food."

"I have my bag already."

"I bet, greedy."

"So, what's up with grandma?" I asked as we made our way back into the living room.

"What do you mean?"

"She didn't say anything to me. I tried talking to her, but she walked away from me."

"Really?"

"Yeah."

"That's weird. She hasn't said anything to me about you. When's the last time you saw her?"

"When I moved out."

"Um, well, that's probably why, Tamar."

"What? I've been busy. Trying to get settled into a new place is draining."

"Yeah but you can still make time to at least call her and see how she's doing."

"Yeah, you're right."

"That weave must be too tight, got you acting crazy."

"Did you really have to go there?"

"Yeah, actually I did. And what's up with you wearing a weave anyway?" she asked.

"Is that a hypothetical question? I'm clearly wearing it because I want to."

"No, it's not a hypothetical question. I want to know when you started wanting to wear a weave. That's not like you."

"Well obviously it is since I'm wearing one."

"Whoa. Time out with the attitude please. I'm not really ready for all of that."

"I don't have an attitude. You're being rude, Hannah."

"And you're not being yourself. Ever since you started working for this company, Tamar, you've changed. You changed the way you dress, the way you wear your hair. I haven't even seen you at church in a while. What's up with that?"

"I told you. I've been busy getting settled into my new place."

"And what about the hair? The clothes?"

"What's wrong with my clothes?"

"I've never seen you dress the way you have the last couple of months. You're wearing four and five inch heels, form fitting dresses, and tight jeans. What's that all about?"

"I've grown up. I've switched up my style. What's wrong with that?"

"Nothing, as long as you're doing it because you want to, and not because you're trying to be like the women you work with."

"Excuse me?"

"I'm just saying. You were telling me about the way they dress and now you're starting to dress like them. I hope you're not doing it to fit it with your colleagues. You don't have to conform to their ways, Tamar."

"I know that, Hannah. I wanted to look like a 25 year-old adult so I switched up my wardrobe. What's the problem in that?"

"Nothing at all. You just look, you know, different."

"Different like how?"

"Different like, well…you look like mom."

"Okay, so I'm going to go home because you're tripping. I love you. Kiss my niece and nephew for me. Have a good night."

"Why are you walking away? I'm just trying to understand you."

"Goodnight, Hannah."

I grabbed my bag of food, my purse and I left. I drove home so fast I thought I'd get a ticket. Hannah really made me mad. I didn't want to say anything disrespectful to my sister so I thought it was best that I left. She's clearly being a hater and I don't have time to be criticized by her. First my grandmother, then Miriam, and now Hannah. I feel like all of the people I love are turning their backs on me just because I've changed. And then she added insult to injury by saying that I look like Eve. I don't look like that woman. I hate her and she knows it. Why would she say that to me?

I poured myself a glass of wine as soon as I got inside my condo. I stood in my living room and looked out of the window at the Bay Bridge. I should be so happy right now. Not many women from Richmond can say they have a college degree, no kids, make sixty thousand dollars a year, and have a condo overlooking the ocean. Why isn't my family happy for me? Why do I care? I closed my eyes, let out a heavy sigh and sat my glass down. I felt some kind of way about my grandmother ignoring me and my sister basically telling me that I'm being a follower. What's so wrong with me growing? Or wanting to dress, behave and live like a grown woman? That's all that I'm doing.

I've lived with my grandmother my entire life. I've done everything that she demanded of me. I just want to figure out who I am as a woman. It's not like I had my own mother around to teach me how to be a woman. Since my mother is in prison for killing my father, who was her pimp, I really don't know who I am. I don't see anything wrong with me wanting to come home after work and keep to myself. I've always attended to my grandmother when I lived with her. I'm just enjoying the break, that's all. I don't know why they're making a big deal about it.

I finished my glass of wine, cleaned my condo and took a hot bath. I dozed off in the tub listening to Kierra Sheard. I woke up to hearing her singing her heart out on Praise Offering. It was pretty late when I crawled into bed, so I turned the TV on to watch a few episodes of Devious Maids. If I wake up on time, I'll try to make it church. If not, I'll be catching Matthew Stevenson on YouTube instead. I'll probably do that anyway to avoid seeing the people who are angry with me. As long as I hear the Word that's fine with me. I'll send my tithes in the mail again.

Although one of my favorite shows was playing, I was distracted by the conversation I had with my sister. I touched my hair and glanced over at the closet where my new clothes were hanging. I am definitely not the same person I was when I started working, and I'm honestly not sure if that's a good or a bad thing right now. Maybe Hannah is right. Am I conforming to the world? Or am I just acting like Eve?

Honestly, I'd do almost anything to have a relationship with my mom. I need my mom. Who else can teach me how to navigate through this cold world? Who else can teach me how to be confident in the skin that I'm in?

Yes, my grandmother taught me things, but I feel like she hid a lot from me because she was afraid I'd be like her daughter. I'm not saying I wanted to run the streets when I was younger, but I wouldn't have minded being taught how to dress, or how to do my hair, or how to put on make-up. I would have loved to have conversations about men, go shopping with my mom, and just have that mother-daughter time.

My grandmother kept us in church and that's it. She did nothing maternal with us, nothing at all. The only thing she taught me was how to cook, pray and keep my legs closed.

I didn't realize how much it bothered me until now. Whatever. It is what it is. I'm going to live my life to the best of my ability. I'm not bending over backwards to please my grandmother or my sister. I'm going to do whatever I want to do. And if they have a problem with it, they can stay out of my life the same way they're staying out of Eve's life.

Seven

The last few weeks have been so crazy busy for me. I've been working longer hours and really haven't had any me time. I'm honestly overwhelmed. Work to my personal life things were moving along at a fast pace. We were closing deals faster than we could even celebrate. And lately I've been traveling with Richard, so my personal life has been really suffering. I actually don't have one anymore.

While work has been going really great, my personal life has been all bad. My grandma still isn't talking to me and things are still shaky with me and Miriam, and Hannah isn't feeling me too much right about now. They all think I'm getting out of control, whatever that means. All of my loving relationships are on pause right now. And, of course, I'm still single.

My relationship with God is even on the brinks of failure. I haven't been to church in over three months. I haven't been praying as much as I should, I stopped tithing, and I haven't been reading my bible as much. I've been doing everything but giving God glory. I'm really pretty ashamed, more so when I hear it from Hannah; she makes it a point to remind me of exactly how many Sunday's I've missed whenever I see or talk to her. She truly gets on my nerves.

My alarm went off for the third time and I let out a sigh. I am so glad it's Friday. I definitely need a break. I rolled out of bed, hopped in the shower, put on my robe and strolled to my kitchen. I was dreading every step that I took. I needed some coffee in my system before I made another move.

As I poured cream and sugar into my cup I thought of my grandma. She's usually up this early drinking coffee and watching the news. I bit the corner of my lip and was deep in thought about what I wanted to do. I went back to my room and contemplated calling my grandma. I really did miss talking to her. I took a deep breath and called. I was surprised that she answered, so it took me a while to respond.

"Hello?" she said for the second time.

"Um, hey. Hi, grandma, how are you?"

"I'm okay."

"I haven't talked to you in a while."

"Mmm hmm."

"Everything good?"

"Yeah, I'm just fine."

"Are you mad at me or something?"

"Mad, no. Disappointed, yes. You done let those people down there at that job change who you are and I don't like it."

"Grandma, it's not what you think."

"It's exactly what I think. I see the way you're dressing now and wearing your hair. I saw you at the birthday party. Hannah even showed me some pictures on Faceback or whatever that internet stuff is."

"Facebook."

"Whatever. Walking around here looking, dressing and probably acting like your mama."

"Grandma, please just-,"

"Until you stop working there, dressing like that and wearing that weave, I don't have anything to say to you, young lady."

"Wait a minute, grandma; are you serious?"

"Yes, I am. I love you but I don't like the person you are changing into right now. I've seen your mama going down the same path. She met your daddy, changed into a prostitute and now she's in prison for killing him. I can't do this all over again. I won't let you break my heart, too. I'll keep you in prayer. Be safe and take care of yourself, Tamar."

"Grand-."

My grandma hung up the phone before I could say anything else. I looked at my phone in disbelief and immediately felt the tears falling down my face. I can't believe her! I put away my phone and wiped my face. I was so hurt. I let out a heavy sigh and went to my closet for something quick to put on.

Times like this I really don't like being an adult. Even though my feelings are hurt, I still have to be at work and that's the last place I wanted to be right now. After I slid on an orange midi dress with a tan blazer and a pair of tan pumps, I put on my make-up, grabbed my purse and made my way to the Bart station. I glanced at myself as I walked past the parked cars along the way. I ran my hands through my new wavy weave as I quickly made my way to the gate.

My sister and grandma are right about one thing: I definitely am a new woman. The difference between me and them is that I like the new me.

I almost bumped into some guy as I was pulling my ticket out of my purse. I had to quickly close my mouth before I started to drool. He was the most handsome man I've seen in a long time. I welcomed the handsome distraction.

"Excuse me, I'm…I'm sorry."

"No problem, beautiful. After you."

The handsome man stood to the side and let me insert my ticket into the machine. I quickly headed towards the escalator once I made it through the gate. I noticed that the handsome man was heading in the same direction as I was. I felt myself becoming nervous, or maybe I was anxious? Maybe I was a little of both, I don't know, but I definitely felt some kind of way.

I could see Sasha was standing on the platform when I reached the top of the escalator. I let out a sigh of relief, smiled at my friend, looked over my shoulder and raised my freshly waxed eyebrows. Sasha smiled and licked her lips. I shook my head. Sasha is a hot mess.

"Hello, handsome," she said to him.

"Hello to you, beautiful."

"How are you?"

"Not too bad, I can't complain. How are you this morning?"

"Oh, I'm fine."

I turned away and checked to see if the train was coming. Sasha cleared her throat and that is when I saw she was blinking her eyes at me fast. I looked at the handsome man standing between us and saw that he was staring at me. I felt butterflies as soon as we locked eyes.

"Since you almost knocked me over, you might as well tell me who you are. What's your name?" he asked.

"Tamar and I'm sorry about that."

"I'm Patrick and I accept your apology, Tamar."

"Thanks." I let out a nervous laugh.

"No worries. You can bump into me anytime. It's nice to meet you, Tamar."

"Likewise."

Patrick lingered a little while longer before he spoke again. "Can I give you my number?" He asked.

"Um, sure."

"I would love to take you out to dinner."

"That would be nice." Patrick gave me his business card.

"Good, I'm already looking forward to it. Enjoy your day, Tamar."

"You, too, Patrick."

Patrick walked down to the next car while Sasha and I loaded unto the car that stopped in front of us. Sasha found two men who offered to give up their seats so we sat down. She couldn't wait to ask me about Patrick.

"Where did that fine piece of a man come from?" she asked.

"I accidentally ran into him when I was walking through the gate."

"You sure you did it on accident?"

"Yeah, I'm sure. I think."

"Mmm hmm. Well, good. You finally can have some company in that beautiful condo of yours. If I lived there, I would have had at least five complaints from my neighbors by now."

"Oh my gosh, I don't even want to know what the complaints would be."

"You sure?"

"And I'm still not having any company so don't start that."

"Why not? It's the weekend. You're single. Have some fun, doll."

"Sasha, no. That is not my style. I'm waiting for something with some substance. I'm waiting for love."

"Girl, you're going to be waiting forever. Just go out with the man and let him spend his money on a nice dinner. You deserve to be wined and dined."

"I'll think about it."

"You're always thinking about something, how about you do something. Doesn't that sound like more fun?"

"Yeah, sure."

"Whatever, boring Betty." She stuck her tongue out at me.

I couldn't tell Sasha that the real reason I haven't had a man over to my place is because I'm a virgin. I don't know what she'd think about me if she knew. Being a 25 year-old virgin would definitely make me the joke of the office and I wasn't about to let anyone in on that joke. We're cool and all, but I wasn't ready to let her know that about me just yet.

Sasha and I finally made it to work and we made plans to meet for lunch at 12:30. Sasha took a selfie of us and posted it to Instagram before we went our separate ways. That girl loves her some social media. I still haven't falling in love with it, I just flirt with it.

When I made it to my desk I frowned because I was surprised to find Richard here. He never comes in before nine but he was here early today. Something big must be going on and that made me nervous. I put my purse down and walked into his office to see why he was here so early. I knocked on his door before I slowly opened it.

"Hey, good morning Richard. You're here early. Is everything okay?" I asked.

"Hey, um, well no, I guess not. I got a call from my new client who confirmed his meeting today and I thought it was next Friday."

"Oh no, did I forget to put him on the calendar?"

"No, I forgot that he does whatever he wants. He changed the meeting at the last minute."

"So why didn't you tell him he has to stick to his original meeting?"

"I guess you don't want any new money in your life, but I do."

"Um, okay, whatever that means. Well, what can I do?"

"Well the first thing you can do is get rid of the sarcasm. Second, he'll be here at ten. Set up the conference room, and draw up the contract based off of the documents that I emailed you a few minutes ago. Everything else on our agenda can wait. If I have any other meetings for today, cancel them. I need you to be on point today. I don't want him to know that we are stressing out over this. He can bring us in some big money, so let's do our thing in there today, okay?"

"Okay, I'm on it."

I went back to my desk and quickly drew up the contract. I gathered all of the documents I would need for the meeting and put them in folders. I called our lawyer to make sure he'd be available to discuss any questions the client might have. I viewed the clients file to see what his requests were so that they'd be available to him when he arrived. I saw that the new client's name was Lucas Christoph. I heard that name before. I immediately thought about Sasha. She mentioned him to me a few weeks ago.

Lucas Christoph is the CEO of one of the fastest growing internet startup companies in Silicon Valley. He's rich, he's smart, he's fine and he's single. I had to let my girl know that he was coming into the office. She's always talking about wanting a fine, rich man. I wanted to see if she'd bag this one.

I finished printing out what I needed for the impromptu meeting and headed over to Sasha's office and burst right in without knocking. I hope that she didn't have a client.

"Sasha!"

"Tamar!"

"Guess who our client is today?"

"Who, girl?"

"Lucas Christoph."

"Lucas Christoph! As in the internet startup baller?"

"Yep, that Lucas."

"Girl, don't play with me!'

"I'm so serious! I was confirming his file and saw his name and profile. He'll be here any minute."

"Oh, my gosh, for real?"

"For real."

"Now you know I'm about to bag that! Okay get out. I need to freshen up my make-up."

"You too funny," I said, laughing.

"No, I'm too serious."

"I see. Bye, girl."

I went back to my desk and quickly checked my emails. I replied to a few urgent messages before heading to the meeting. I grabbed the documents I needed, went into the conference room and quickly scanned the room to make sure everything was in place before I went back to my desk to start on a project one of Richard's associates asked me to work on. Richard kept calling me into his office to help him do things for the upcoming meeting, so I barely got anything done.

My phone rang and I promptly answered it.

"Richard White's office, Tamar speaking, how can I assist you?"

"You can assist me by quitting that job and giving your life back to Christ."

I was surprised to hear my sister on the other end of the call. I was wondering why she didn't call my cell phone.

"Excuse me?"

"It's me, Tamar. Hannah."

"I know who it is. Why didn't you call my cell?"

"Because you wouldn't have answered."

"Good point. What do you want? I'm working."

"We need to talk."

"Hannah, I'm not in the mood. I'm busy and I'm focused on work. I can't with you right now."

"This is not about me. This is about your salvation. You're losing it because of this new person you've become."

"If you're going to preach to me, I can tell you right now. I won't be talking to you. Talk to me like an adult and I'll consider it."

"Lord, I'm asking that you release Tamar from the spirit of anger. I pray that you-."

I hung up the phone on my sister in the midst of her prayer and finished checking my emails. I am not in the mood for a deliverance prayer. Like I said, I can't do her right now.

I'm trying to work and here she goes wanting to be an intercessor. Nope, not today.

The reminder for my upcoming meeting flashed across my screen and I gathered my materials and headed to the conference room. As I was setting up, Lucas Christoph was walking in with two other guys. I couldn't believe my eyes. All of the men were very attractive. I smelled three different scents of cologne and they all smelled so good. I could feel a pair of eyes on me but was too afraid to make eye contact. I introduced myself and led the men into our conference room. I had to ask God to forgive me for the thoughts that crept into my mind because they weren't holy, pure or righteous at all.

I sat in the meeting extremely impressed by the businessmen I was surrounded by. As I listened to the men talk business, I could see why women were attracted to Lucas. He's very intelligent, extremely well spoken, and listening to the figures they were talking, his money is very long. I had to admit that I was very intrigued.

Every now and then Lucas would motion for me to pour him more water, and his partner kept asking for coffee. I could feel his partner staring me down every time I received signatures for the documents. I see why women feel like meat around aggressive businessmen. They certainly treat us like so. I tugged at my dress a little before I sat down and I locked eyes with Lucas' business partner. He was grinning and licking his lips at me. Surprisingly, I felt myself blush. I couldn't believe myself. Lucas' partner licking his lips did something to me and I don't know why I liked that. I was embarrassed because he saw me while he simply chuckled and sipped his coffee. I'll be glad when this meeting is over. I need to pray again.

Once the meeting was over, I shook Lucas' business partner's hand and told Lucas to have a good day. Lucas asked Richard to stay while I exited the conference room. I ran my hand that shook the partner's hand across my one of my hips and smiled. I couldn't believe a man's touch made me feel like that. I've never had that happen to me before and it scared me because I liked it. Oh, Lord, please don't strike me down.

As I tried to process what I was feeling, I called Sasha to tell her that our meeting was over. Just as I was hanging up the phone, the men walked out of the conference room. The smirk on Richard's face let me know that I wouldn't have to probe about what was discussed because he'll, in fact, tell me as soon as he got a free moment.

Richard was briskly walking with Lucas' business partner towards my desk. I did not like the sneaky look on Richard's face, so I pretended that I was busy reading an email when they were getting closer to my desk. I immediately felt my stomach knot up and let out a shaky sigh. Richard was grinning and raising his eyebrows at me when I looked up. I forced myself to smile.

"Tamar, this is Jeff. Lucas' business partner. Jeff, this is my lovely assistant, Tamar."

"Hello, Jeff, nice to meet you."

"It's very nice to meet you, Tamar."

"I'll leave you two alone." Richard nodded and went into his office. My eyes followed Richard trying to get his attention, but he didn't look in my direction. I couldn't believe him!

"So," Jeff said. "Are you single, Tamar?" he asked. He got straight to the point. He was clearly bold and a total opposite of who I am.

"Um, yes. Yes, I am."

"Great! So it shouldn't be a problem if I wanted to take you out to dinner tonight, right?"

"Um, I don't know."

"Well, think about it. Here's my card." Jeff placed the fancy business card on my desk. "Call me when you decide what you want to do. Cool?"

"Yeah. Sure, that's cool."

"Have a good day, Ms. Lady."

"You, too."

Richard came out a few moments after Jeff left my desk to make sure they were out of the office. It was almost like he timed it. He watched Lucas and his team leave, tapped my desk as he walked by and went into his office. I heard Richard laugh before he asked me to come into his office. He eagerly told me to shut the door and have a seat. I gave Richard the side eye as I sat down since he kept grinning at me.

"Tamar, Tamar, Tamar. I told you that make-over would work in our favor. Jeff is very interested in you and wanted to know if it would be a conflict of interest if you two went out. Of course I said it wouldn't be."

"Say what?"

"Yes. You can let him take you out, use that time to butter him up and get him to sign that contract on Monday. I'll give you money to buy yourself the most seductive dress you can find and take him to the finest restaurant the Bay has to offer. Use that magic God gave you women to talk us out of every penny we have."

"Excuse me?"

"Let's get this money, Tamar."

"Richard, you cannot be serious right now."

"Oh, I'm very serious. If Lucas signs that contract, we'll be ten million dollars richer. And if Lucas' business partner is feeling my assistant, I mean, well, that's common sense, Tamar."

"I mean, you like, have no filter whatsoever."

"Should I?"

"Yeah, yeah you really should."

"I don't have time for all of that. I need that contract, Tamar, and you're the one to see fit that I get it."

"Whoa, wait a minute now! That's way too much pressure, Richard, and I'm not comfortable doing that. That's not my style."

"Well do whatever you're comfortable with doing as long as it makes him want to sign that contract as is. Finish up your day so you can get ready for your date."

"I don't have a date."

"You sure do. He's asked you out."

"And who said I'd go?"

"I did. Your job depends on it. Now get out of here and get dolled up."

Richard dismissed me with an arrogant fling of his hand. He turned his attention towards his computer screen, leaving me to feel like an idiot. I sighed, got up and stomped out of Richard's office. He sent me an instant message saying I'll get over my attitude after he deposits a bonus of five thousand dollars into my checking account once the contract is signed. I read that message seven times before I accepted what the words said.

Five thousand, huh?

Yeah, I think he's right about that. I will definitely get over myself for an extra five thousand in my checking account. I thought about what I will do with the money once we get the account and shook my head at myself. Who have I become? My sister would disown me if she knew what I was about to do, which is why she'll never find out.

Since Richard cancelled all of his meetings for the day I really didn't have much work to do anyway. That was a good thing because after the conversation I had with Richard, I could barely concentrate. I do not like that Richard treats me like a signing bonus to the clients. This has been happening over the last few weeks and it's starting to truly bother me. Ever since I switched up my wardrobe, he's been offering me up as if I'm a piece of candy. Yes, he compensates me but now I'm starting to feel like someone and something that I am not, and I don't like it. Okay, well, I don't like it at first, but I totally forget about how I felt when he gives me money.

I didn't want to lose my job so I reluctantly decided I'd go out with Jeff. Since Richard was forcing me to go, per se, I took him up on his offer to buy me a new dress. I stood in his office, pouting and sticking my hand out for his credit card. He smiled at me, told me to do well and kissed my cheek. He's such an arrogant jerk. I hate and love him at the same time.

Once I finished handling all of the things that couldn't wait until Monday, I shut down my desk, said 'goodbye' to Richard and stopped by Sasha's office. She was on the phone, walking back and forth talking with her hands as she tried to close a deal. She motioned for me to come in. I listened as my girl used her mouthpiece skills she got from the streets of Oakland to close a business deal.

Sasha sat back down at her computer and started typing and squirming in her seat. She mouthed the words, 'got him,' winked and ended her call.

"Got another client girl! He'll be in here Tuesday to sign them papers."

"You go, girl!"

"And I bagged Lucas. Ha! We're going out tonight. Maybe we can double date. His assistant was a cutie pie."

"Yeah, he told Richard he wants to take me out, so Richard is pimping me out again. He gave me his card to buy something to wear tonight."

"Dang! I should have been his assistant, I really should have."

"Hush and come on. Let's go to Union Square."

Sasha closed down her office and headed out with me. I was torn about my situation. On one hand it felt good to go shopping with someone else's credit card, but on the other, I did not like the feeling that I was being used as a pawn in a business deal. Sasha picked up on my mood and interrupted my thoughts.

"What's wrong with you, doll?" she asked, trying on a pair of Dior pumps.

"The same thing that's been wrong with me for the last few weeks."

"You still bugging about Richard? Girl, I told you how he gets down and he's not going to change. Whenever you get the courage to quit, he's going to do the same thing to the next woman who works here."

"You think I'll quit?" I asked.

"Yeah because you actually have a conscious, unlike the rest of us who work here. Oh, try these on. If he's treating, you may as well get the best they have to offer."

Sasha handed me a pair of beautiful Christian Louboutin's. I can't even front and say that I didn't fall in love with them. They were just my style, peep-toe with a platform. I tried on the pretty shoes and walked around in them for a few seconds. I took them off and gave them to the cashier. I whipped Richard's credit card out so fast I almost broke my wrist. I don't have a problem spending his money at all. Sasha has definitely rubbed off on me.

"So I'm going out with Jeff tonight and I'm nervous," I said to Sasha, searching for a dress to match my shoes.

"Why?"

"I don't want him to think I'm going to sleep with him."

"You don't have to, just make him think that you will."

"Huh?"

"Look, flirt and tease the man all night long and get him really drunk and kick him to the curb."

"Girl, I am not doing that."

"Why not?"

"No, Sasha."

"Okay, well pull the oldest trick in the book."

"What's that?"

"Tell him it's that time of the month."

"I knew I liked you for a reason."

"Thanks, doll."

After three hours of shopping for the perfect outfit, Sasha and I headed back to Oakland. I was as ready for my night with Jeff as I could be. Once I received a call from Jeff confirming our plans for the evening, I gave him my address and he told me to be ready by seven. I looked at my phone for the time and sighed. I had four hours to get ready. That should be plenty of time for me to take a quick nap and attempt to pray. That is, if I could stop feeling guilty enough to approach God's throne and ask for some guidance.

My cell phone alarm woke me up from my nap and I threw my arm over my face. I was dreading going on this date with Jeff. I really didn't want to go, especially after the way Richard acted when he found out Jeff wanted to take me out.

I know that men often expect women to have sex with them when they take them to an expensive restaurant, but I didn't really want to be put into an awkward situation. I may have compromised my wardrobe, but I will not exchange my virginity for a business deal. That's where I draw the line. I'm really praying that Jeff isn't a jerk.

I turned on Pandora and listened to Beyoncé as I got dressed. I realized that I was singing along to a Beyoncé song and shook my head. I don't even listen to the same music anymore. I have definitely changed.

Jeff was due to pick me up in an hour, so I showered, dressed and styled my weave. I was putting on my makeup when Jeff called to tell me he was downstairs. I let out a nervous sigh, grabbed my purse and keys and headed downstairs to greet him.

I was impressed to find Jeff waiting for me with flowers. That truly changed the mood. He was smiling and looking at me like I was the best thing since fried chicken.

"Aw, flowers, you're so sweet."

"And you're so beautiful." Jeff handed me the flowers and kissed my hand. "How are you?"

"Much better."

"Were you nervous?" he asked.

"Still am."

"No need to be. I'm just a regular guy who wants to take a beautiful woman out for some fun, that's all."

"Sounds good."

"Do you want to put these in water? I'll wait right here."

"Um, sure, I'll be right back." I quickly headed upstairs, put the flowers down and exhaled. When I made it back downstairs, Jeff was holding the car door open for me. I was so impressed with his mannerisms.

Jeff took me to some fancy seafood restaurant and showed me the typical rich guy, arrogant attitude. Although he was arrogant, he was actually a nice guy. He's just used to getting what he wants; must be nice.

After dinner, we went to a lounge and listened to a live band that a friend of his was the lead singer. The guy invited us to an after party and I had a ball. We danced and drank champagne and danced some more. Jeff really showed me a good time.

There was a few times where he got a little too touchy feely for me, and when he did, I eased back and smiled, telling him to be patient with my eyes. He'd nod, laugh and kiss my hand.

It was well after midnight when we made it back to my place. Jeff asked me if he could come up for a while and I hesitated. I didn't want to give off the impression that we'd sleep together but I quickly remembered my job depended on how I finished this night.

I decided I'd pour us both a glass of wine, put on a movie and fall asleep. I was so glad that my plan worked because that is exactly what happened. Jeff must have been tired as well because he fell asleep before I did.

Jeff was sound asleep on my couch while I stood in my kitchen asking God to forgive me for allowing a man, who will never be my husband, to sleep under the same roof as me. I really needed to go to church, fall down on my face and repent.

Maybe next Sunday.

Eight

"What are you doing?"

"Um, sleeping. What are you doing?"

"About to come pick you up."

"Wait, what?"

"Yes. Get up, wash the cakes and get dressed. Lucas is taking us to brunch. I'll be there in thirty minutes. Bye!"

I looked at the phone, shook my head and smiled. Leave it up to Sasha to have me wilding out on a Sunday morning. I rubbed my eyes and looked at the clock. It was a quarter to ten. I don't have to ask to know that Sasha was already with Lucas. How I got invited is beyond me. I was hoping that Jeff wouldn't be there since I'm not in the mood to pretend to be interested in him right now.

I hopped in the shower, put on my robe and searched my closet for something quick to throw on. I was still in my robe when Sasha rang the bell for me to buzz her in. I wasn't even fully awake yet. I rubbed my eyes and dragged myself to the door. I smiled when I saw Sasha looking fly in a pair of ripped jeans, a tank top and wedges. She had about ten bangles on her wrist and a pair of gold hoops in her ears. I absolutely love her style.

"Really, Tamar?"

"What?"

"Why aren't you dressed?"

"Chill, I just got out of the shower."

"Heffa, get dressed. Lucas and his friend is meeting us at HS Lordship in twenty minutes."

"Okay, okay. I'm just about to throw on my romper. Relax."

"The black one?" she asked.

"Yes."

"Yes, doll! Rock that! You look hot in that thing. Give his friend something to look at besides the waffles."

"No, Sasha. I'm not playing the eye candy role today."

"Why not, doll? You already have the sweets. Look at that booty." Sasha smacked me on the butt. "That's a candy store all by itself."

"I can't stand you."

"You love me."

"And who is his friend?" I asked, slipping into my outfit.

"Some boss I met last night."

"Not Jeff?"

"No."

"Sasha."

"I know you went out with the corny business partner, but this guy is the one you need to bag. I can tell he likes spending his money on pretty women."

"Please don't start that, Sasha. You know I don't get down like that."

"Keep hanging with me and you'll be getting up, down and around just like that."

"Oh gosh!"

Ten minutes later I was sitting in the passenger seat of Sasha's coupe singing along to a Rihanna song. If Miriam or

Hannah knew that I actually knew the words to a Rihanna song, they would throw holy water and oil on me and rebuke whatever demon that jumped on me in the name of Jesus.

Lucas and a tall, well dressed, handsome guy were standing out front waiting for us when we arrived. The biggest smile appeared on Lucas' face when he saw Sasha. I guess he fell under her spell because he was very happy to see her. She kissed him, shook his friend's hand and introduced us.

"Devin, this is Tamar. Tamar, Devin."

"Nice to meet you," I said, shaking Devin's hand.

"Likewise."

Sasha led the way and we were seated shortly after going inside the restaurant. We ordered mimosa's, toasted to new friendships and went our separate ways to the buffet. Devin and I locked eyes a time or two. His smile was very mesmerizing. Very. I ignored that mushy feeling in the pit of my stomach and stacked my plate with French toast, eggs, bacon and fruit.

Lucas and Sasha were already at the table when I returned from the buffet. They were all over each other so

I'm not sure why Devin and I were even invited. They paid us no attention whatsoever.

Devin took it upon himself to ease the awkward silence between us. He was charismatic, attentive and funny, not shy at all. I was glad that he wasn't because I haven't learned how to be as outspoken as Sasha.

"So, you work with Sasha, correct?" he asked.

"Um, yes. I'm an executive assistant to one of the managers in our company."

"Nice, so you're his right hand woman. Keep him on track."

"That's exactly what I do. What about you?" I asked.

"I own a real estate company, a restaurant and two barbershops."

"Oh, so you're a boss. Nice."

He smiled. "Something like that."

"So are you single, Devin?"

"I sure am. Do you think I'd be out on a Sunday morning trying to get to know you if I wasn't?"

"Not sure, have to be certain these days."

"I see. What about you?" he asked.

"Very single."

"Is that different from just regular old single?"

"Very." We laughed.

"You're beautiful."

"Thanks and you're handsome."

"I know."

"What?"

He chuckled. "I'm joking."

"I was about to say!"

"It's hard to believe that you're single. Is that by choice?"

"Pretty much. I'm just trying to stay focused on work. What about you?"

"No, not by choice. I don't want a woman to use me for my money. It's hard to meet women who are genuinely interested in me. Most women see me and see dollar signs."

"Really? I just see a man eating some waffles."

"Funny."

"Seriously, I understand. I'm sure that must be hard."

"Yep. It is. I would love to be in a committed relationship. I enjoy spending my time with someone special."

"Yeah. I guess so."

"What? You don't want to be married or in a relationship?" he asked.

"Sure, I just want him to be right for me."

"I see. Do you date?"

"No."

"So how can you know if someone is right for you?"

"Good question. When I find out I'll let you know."

"Do you want to date?"

"Yes, I do."

"Well maybe you can start with me."

"Maybe."

After brunch, we all hopped in the car with Lucas and went to the City. We hit up Pier 39, went to a museum, did a little shopping and just chilled. I had a great time with Devin even after he told me how accomplished he was. I thought he'd be stuck up and arrogant, but he was so humble. I actually forgot that he was rich. However, I was reminded of how rich he was when he started paying for everything.

Anytime Devin pulled out his credit card to pay, I found myself wanting to decline and pay for myself, but Sasha would give me a look that said 'if I opened my mouth she was going to go East Oakland on me.' I didn't want that so I let him pay. We finally ended our day with dinner and Lucas took us back to Sasha's car.

"I really enjoyed hanging out with you today," Devin said, smiling and playing with my hands.

"Me, too. You weren't as stuck up or arrogant as I thought."

"Funny girl I see."

"Sometimes."

"Do we have to go our separate ways yet? I would love to keep chilling with you."

"Um." I looked at Sasha and she was non-verbally telling me not to end the night. I was so nervous. I didn't want to because I liked talking to Devin, but I'm old enough to know that Devin didn't want to just talk to me. He was attracted to me. Devin wanted to talk to my body and I wasn't ready for that. I also wasn't ready for us to go our separate ways. What's a girl to do?

"Well?" he asked.

"What did you have in mind?"

"Netflix and chill?"

"Oh gosh!"

"Seriously, whatever you want. I just don't want to leave your presence."

"Charming I see."

"Is it working?"

"Yes, it's working. Come on, follow us to my place and I'll take you home."

I was so nervous on the short drive to my place. Sasha was saying something to me but I didn't even acknowledge her. I was trying to think of how I was going to get around saving my virginity. I liked Devin but not enough to give him the most precious thing that I have.

Before Devin and I went upstairs we got into my car and went to Trader Joe's for wine, popcorn, cheese and fruit. Once we made it back to my place, I decided to reiterate to Devin that I didn't want to have sex. I just wanted to hang out. I was hoping he wouldn't turn into a psycho after I said what I wanted to say. I've watched enough of those shows on the ID channel and I was not trying to be on the next episode of any of those shows.

Devin opened the wine and poured the sweet white drink into glasses. I popped popcorn and put some fruit and cheese on a platter. While Devin searched for a movie to watch, I gave my spiel.

"So, um, Devin, I really like you and enjoy talking to you, but I don't want you to have any expectations that we're going to have sex."

"Is that why you think I wanted to hang out with you?" he asked.

"Well, I don't know and I certainly don't want to assume, so I just wanted to be clear."

"I'm shocked that you would think you can have some of this on the first date."

"Excuse me?"

"You can't have my body on the first date, Tamar. I have to get to know you first, young lady."

"Oh, so I can't have none of your body?" I asked.

"Nope. I mean, I know I'm all fine and everything, but I'm off limits the first ninety days. Steve Harvey taught me the rules. I know what's up."

. "Omg! You're hella funny."

"Seriously, Tamar, I have no expectations. I like you. I like talking to you. I didn't want the night to end. That's all. After we watch a movie, I'll leave. You don't even have to take me, I'll call an Uber."

"No, you're my guest. I don't mind."

"Good. Now that we cleared the air, pass the popcorn."

I was glad that we were able to talk and I didn't feel any pressure to do anything that I didn't want to do. Devin is the perfect gentleman and I love it. He's so easy to talk to. I really hope that we can be friends. I relaxed, enjoyed my wine and Devin's company.

I don't know when we stopped watching the movie or at what point we finished the two bottles of wine or when we made it to my bedroom. I just know that I woke up the next morning with Devin in my bed and a smile on my face.

Devin and I were having breakfast when I received a barrage of text messages from Hannah with different bible verses about repentance. I was two point five seconds away from getting mad but the verses she sent were pretty good.

After breakfast Devin left and I hopped in the shower, then threw on my sweats to relax. I received a call from Miriam but decided to ignore her. The last few times we've talked was strained and I wasn't in the mood to pretend with her today. Then Hannah called. Now I was getting annoyed and I ignored her call also. I poured myself a glass of wine and started watching an episode of Shameless.

When I heard my doorbell ring a half hour later, I was annoyed even more. One, I wasn't expecting anyone; and two, someone was interrupting my show, Shameless. I looked out of the window to see if I saw any familiar cars in the visitors section. I rolled my eyes when I saw Hannah's Lexus. I let out a sigh, sat my glass of wine down and buzzed her in. A few seconds later Hannah was knocking on my door. She wasn't alone. Miriam was in tow.

"Why are you here?" I asked.

"Well hello to you too, sister. How are you? I'm fine. Thanks so much for asking."

"I'm not about to pretend that I'm happy to see you or her. What do you want, Hannah?"

"Oh no, you're about to put that funky little worldly attitude of yours on pause. We are here as your sisters in Christ and we are calling you out for your behavior as of late."

"Really, Hannah? Really?"

"Yes, really. Ya'll have known each other since you were ten years old. I don't know what's going on, but it needs to stop."

"This is none of your business, Hannah."

"Now it is."

"Don't you have some kids to raise and a husband to attend to?" I asked.

"Girl, you really need to chill with all of that attitude. I'm not one of your little friends. I don't mind smacking you, Tamar."

"Hannah, I'm not a little girl and I can promise you, if you put your hands on me, you're going to be sorry."

"What?" Hannah dropped her purse on the couch and walked in my direction. Miriam jumped in between us.

"Whoa, chill out ladies. I didn't come over here for this. Tamar, why are you ignoring me? What have I done?"

"I don't have to explain myself to you."

"I never asked you to. I just wanted to check on you. The last time I saw you..."

"The last time you saw me I was having a good time and you had to go and ruin it by calling on the blood of Jesus at a party. Do you know how embarrassing that is?"

"Hold up…you're mad because I prayed for you? You know what, you seriously have some issues. I don't know what you've been doing at that job, but that place has got you twisted."

"I've been getting money. Something you know nothing about."

"Don't flatter yourself because you're making a few dollars. You may as well be a stripper or a prostitute since your boss is basically your pimp."

"Get the hell out of my house. Now!"

"Fine. I'm done. I'll be in the car," Miriam told Hannah on her way out the door.

"Tamar, you're tripping. I don't know what your problem is, but you need to get it together. And fast." Hannah shook her head, grabbed her purse and left. I locked the door and stormed to my room. I was so mad I couldn't even think straight. I paced back and forth, huffing and puffing, trying to understand what just happened.

Nine

There's no denying that since I've started working for Richard my life has done a complete one-eighty. I'm a brand new woman with a different perspective on life and I love the new me.

I've been transformed from a boring church girl to a woman of the world. Not to throw shade at church girls but it's true. I know I should repent and give my heart back to God, but if I can be real for two point five seconds, I'm not ready quite yet. I'm enjoying myself.

I'm not used to men wanting to go out with me. I'm not used to having friends who like to have fun outside of church or listen to R&B or dress like divas. I've been introduced to a new side of life and I like what I've learned so far.

I just hope that God will forgive me when I turn back to the path of righteousness. I hope that he understands that I just want to have fun, enjoy life. I still love Him, I just want to do my own thing for a while. I don't want to be a part of the world forever, I just wanted to see what all of the hoopla was about and now that I know, I understand.

Before meeting Sasha and working for Richard, I wasn't happy. I was living with my grandmother, working at a restaurant and had no action from the brothers. Now I have a career, my own place and men now find me attractive. Yes, I like the woman I've become despite what my family and old friends think about me. I am finally happy and I love my life.

The woman that I've allowed Richard and my friendship with Sasha mold me into is excited about the future. I've learned so much about myself and I feel like I'll be much better when I repent. I just really hope that my family will feel the same, especially my grandmother.

My grandmother can barely stand the sight of me anymore. She just looks at me and shakes her head whenever she sees me, which is far and in between because it's just too awkward. She told me that she doesn't even recognize me anymore. She says I look and act just like Eve now. That really hurt my feelings. We were so close but now we are estranged. She raised me to be a faithful, holy, pure, sanctified daughter of the Most High and, as of late, I've been everything but. I understand why she doesn't want to see me and that's fine because I'm not going back to being the boring church girl right now anyway. I want to find my own way to live and serve God. I haven't yet so I'll keep my distance.

I haven't been to church or bible study in months and I used to attend both faithfully every single week. I never missed a week and now I don't even go at all. I don't want to be talked about amongst the congregation, so I just watch sermons when I can on YouTube. Besides, I'm sure my grandmother has told sister and brother so and so about how I've turned into a heathen or how I now act like Jezebel. I just can't face my church family knowing that I'm not the person they know me to be.

Working for Richard has forced me to make a few decisions that I'm not very proud of. I can't look my pastor in the face knowing I've done some things he wouldn't approve of. I can't stand in church singing and worshipping knowing that I've lusted after some man I don't even know, let alone isn't married to. I refuse to attend bible study knowing that I've been drinking wine every day for the last six months. I just can't.

Even though I'm aware that some of the things I do for the nice checks I get compromises my beliefs and my relationship with God, I haven't quit working for Richard. I'm living the lifestyle a lot of people wish for. I know that I should quit my job since it's compromising who I am in Christ, but I'm caught up in the fleshly and worldly pleasures I receive. I've grown attached to my lifestyle and I'm having a hard time parting ways with it. I understand why the rich man didn't want to let go of his possessions to follow Jesus. Not that it was right but I'm just saying.

Although I'm living a pretty good life, I know that I'm no longer walking in my divine favor I once was because my life is so different now. I can admit that I am not living the life of how a true daughter of the Most High should. I owe who I've become to my job, not the Most High, and that is not good. I can't even thank Him for what I have because I didn't get this far by being a good person or by walking by faith. I've been walking by sight which is why I've turned into the woman that I am.

My job has changed me and I don't know how to go back to being the woman I was when I first started working for Richard. I don't know if I can stop being this person. I'm honestly not sure that I want to.

Sometimes I sit and reminisce about the way things were before I got a new attitude, new weave and wardrobe.

My family was so proud of everything that I was able to accomplish, especially my sister and grandmother. I still remember the day I got this job. It was a great day in my family.

I had just graduated from San Francisco State off of a full ride, academic scholarship when I got hired. My church family gave me a surprise dinner at my favorite restaurant. All of my family and friends were there and I was so happy, so grateful. Everyone was so proud of me and it felt good. Now no one is talking to me. Whatever. They'll get over it.

My phone rang as I was sliding into a black dress and I let out a sigh. It's Monday morning and I'm not ready to get back to work because I knew it was going to be crazy at the office. With Lucas signing the deal and Richard gloating about it, it's going to be a very long day.

I looked down at the name on the caller ID and answered. It was Sasha.

"Hey, Sasha, what's up?"

"The usual. Which Bart train are you catching today?" she asked.

"The 8:17 at the West Oakland station. Are you going to meet me there?"

"Yep, I'll be there."

"Kay, see you soon."

I hung up the phone and finished getting dressed. I looked at the clock on my wall, saw that I had thirty minutes to get to the station so I wouldn't miss my train and put a pep in my step.

I took one last look at my outfit in the mirror, smiled with approval, grabbed my purse and headed to the Bart station.

My grandmother was on my mind so I dialed her number. She hasn't answered my calls in a few months but I still try to call every week to see if she's had a change of heart.

Nope, she hasn't.

I sighed, put my phone down and found a park since I had arrived at the Bart station. I looked in my rearview mirror and checked my make-up. I looked in my purse for my Clipper card, chirped the alarm on my new Audi coupe and made my way to the platform.

Sasha was already there when I made it up the escalator. She was looking like every bit of the sassy diva she is with her gray high-waisted, pencil skirt and a teal button-up shirt. Her short haircut was fresh and her make-up was flawless. I still can't believe she isn't somebody's model as gorgeous as she is. Her looks is definitely why she's always closing big accounts. That and that mouth piece of hers. She can talk a real good game.

"Good morning, doll; how are you feeling today?" Sasha asked.

"Good morning, I'm pretty good. How are you?"

"Well, seeing that I spent a lot of Lucas' money, I'll have to say I'm great." We shared a laugh.

"You are too funny."

"Don't act brand new. You had fun too, miss thing. How was your night with Devin?" she asked.

"Not what I expected."

"That good or that bad?"

"It was great."

"He put it down, girl?"

"We didn't have sex, Sasha."

"Interesting. So you have no naughty girl shenanigans to tell me about?" she asked.

"Nope, not one."

"Wait, so you were with a millionaire, a fine millionaire might I add, and you didn't pop it on a handstand?"

"No, Sasha, I didn't."

"Girl, you're tripping."

"No, I just have self-respect."

"Please. Self-respect goes out of the window when I know I have a millionaire in my space wanting to spend his money on me."

"I'm not a gold digger thank you."

"I sure am. I'm digging for everything every single time that I catch one: gold, silver, platinum and black cards, too."

"Well, I don't want that kind of karma to come back to me. The bible says you reap what you sow and I don't want to reap that kind of stuff."

"The Lord forgives. So do you, boo."

I shook my head and laughed. "I can't with you."

"Well what was so great about the night if you didn't get it in, doll?" she asked, frowning.

"Wouldn't you like to know?"

"Um, yes!"

"Oh look, here's our train."

She laughed. "Heffa!"

Our Bart train arrived and we squeezed onto the train with the rest of the commuters. I listened as Sasha went into details about her weekend with Lucas. She went into all of the details about the restaurants where they ate, the suite he stayed in, and the clothes he bought her. Meanwhile I'm thinking about the night I spent with Devin. It was so much fun and I can't wait to do it again.

We arrived at our building and went our separate ways. I sat my purse down and put on a pot of coffee. I expected Richard to be there any minute craving for his coffee. He acts like it's crack or something, he's so addicted to caffeine it's not even funny.

I started my day and found myself thinking about Devin. He was one of the nicest men I've ever met. I loved the fact that he accepts me for who I am and doesn't judge me because I like to dress fly, wear weaves and make good money.

I felt my phone vibrate and smiled when I saw the name attached to the text message. It was from Devin. He wanted to have dinner sometime this week, which I agreed to, and squealed when he confirmed a date and time. I was so excited! I'm definitely looking forward to seeing Devin again.

Richard finally arrived to the office as I was typing up the memos from Friday's meeting. He called me into his office.

"Are you ready to close this deal?" he asked.

"Sure, they'll be here in an hour, right?"

"Yes, I wanted to make sure they'll be signing."

"I don't see why not. It's a very lucrative deal, Richard."

"Cool. Where's my coffee?"

"It's not ready."

"What? You started it late?"

"Relax, I just heard the pot. I'll be back."

When I brought Richard his coffee, he informed me that he wants me to attend his out of town meeting next week. He wants me to help him close the deals. I'm sure a shopping spree will be coming. Anytime he says he wants me to help him close a deal, it usually led to me getting a new outfit.

After our meeting with Lucas, Richard gave me his credit card and told me to buy two outfits that will make both clients he's meeting with want to sign with our company. I had no clue what that type of outfit would look like so I went to Sasha's office because she definitely knows.

Sasha was sitting on her desk with her legs crossed, playing with her nails and listening in on a conference call. She motioned for me to sit down. She nodded her head and would chime in on the call every few seconds. Five minutes later she was off of the call and smiling at me.

"Hey, doll, what's up?" she asked.

"Everything. Richard gave me his card again to go shopping. He wants to take me to his out of town meetings next week and told me to get some outfits that will make the clients want to sign with us."

"I know just where to go. You ready now?"

"Sure, let me get my purse."

Sasha led me straight to Neiman Marcus where she found some lady that she knew by name and allowed her to do all of the shopping. We sat down and let her bring us clothes. Sasha did all of the selecting and all I did was try on whatever Sasha picked out. As usual Sasha knew exactly what to get. Everything she picked for me was exactly something Richard would want to see me in. I never would have picked what she picked out. I'm glad I brought her along.

After we left the women's department we stopped by the shoe department and bought heels to match both outfits. Sasha made sure to get herself a couple of pairs, too.

A few hours and a couple thousand dollars later, we were headed back to the Bart station. Since Richard gave me the rest of the day off, Sasha and I went our separate ways when we reached the Bart station in Oakland. I put my bags in the back seat of my car and sat in the parking garage for a few minutes. I wonder how Richard will explain his credit card bill to his wife. Then again, he probably doesn't have to.

My phone rang and Hannah's name and picture illuminated on the screen. I hesitated before answering because I was hoping she wasn't calling me to act like an apostle and preach to me about repenting. I sighed and answered the phone.

"Hey, Hannah, what's up?"

"Not much, how are you?"

"I'm fine. You?"

"Good. I miss my sister, though."

"I miss you, too."

"Come over."

"Today?"

"Yes."

"Is everything okay?" I asked.

"Yeah, why does something have to be wrong for me to invite you over?"

"Just unexpected, that's all. I'm actually off of work. I'm going to stop by my house, change clothes and I'll be over."

"Okay, see you soon."

When I pulled up to Hannah's house, I turned the ignition off and sat in my car. I needed to gather my thoughts before I see my sister. I checked my reflection in the rearview mirror to make sure my make-up was still intact. I wonder how long it will take her to say something about my make-up. She's definitely going to say something about my hair since I'm rocking a long, wavy weave with honey blonde highlights. And she'll say something about my five-inch fancy shoes. I'm really not looking forward to her criticism today.

Hannah popped her head out of the door and waved for me to come in. She had my nephew on her hip and my niece was standing in between her legs. It's crazy seeing my sister as a wife and a mom. I remember when she was still a virgin and singing in the choir, and now she's married with two kids. Life truly amazes me.

"Aunty Tam Tam! Pick me up!" Leah said.

"Hey, beautiful baby girl." I picked my niece up and kissed my nephew.

"Your hair is pretty." Leah rubbed her dirty hands in my hair. I laughed.

"Thank you, baby, so is yours."

"You coming in our house?" she asked.

"Yes, if you let her." Hannah shook her head and made room for me to walk inside. My brother-in-law Mark was on the couch watching Family Feud.

"Hey, Mark, how are you?" I asked.

"Hey, Tamar, I'm pretty good. How's the job going?"

"Oh, it's going. How's the business?"

"Starting to pick up."

"That's good."

"Here, take him. Leah, go clean up those toys please." Hannah passed her baby boy to Mark while Leah went into her room. "Come on, have a seat. You want something to drink?" Hannah asked.

"Yes, water is fine."

"So, what's up with you?"

"Not much, just working. How have you been?"

"Pretty good. I've been missing you."

"I know, I've been missing you, too."

"You did your own make-up?" she asked.

"Yeah. YouTube tutorials are amazing."

"Looks pretty. And your hair?"

"I'm not that good. I got this done at the salon."

"Oh okay."

"What do you have to say?"

"Nothing, nothing at all."

"That's a first."

"I didn't invite you over to argue with you, Tamar."

"Good because I didn't come over for that."

"Have you talked to grandma?"

"I don't know if I want to talk to her."

"What? Tamar that's your grandmother, quit playing."

"I'm just saying, she keeps telling me that I'm acting like Eve. I don't want to hear all of that."

"The truth hurts but that's not an excuse to not talk to her."

"She still won't answer my calls anyway. How is she?"

"She's fine. She misses you."

"I can't tell but I miss her, too."

"You know how stubborn she can be. You should stop by. You know she won't deny you coming inside the house."

"At this point I honestly don't know."

"Stop it. You know better."

"Do I?"

"I don't think you do, especially putting up with that craziness from your boss and dressing the way you do now, but whatever."

"Okay, get it all out now. What else do you want to say?"

"Well, I'm concerned about you, Tamar. You are like a whole new person. The Tamar I know wouldn't dress like this, wear her hair like that or all of that make-up. Or drive that car you drive or live in that expensive condo you have. I just feel like I don't know you anymore."

"I understand your concern, and you're absolutely right; I am not the same Tamar. I feel like I've grown and matured a lot over the last few months and I feel like I needed to. I was a grown woman who looked like a little girl and lived like one, too. I just wanted to feel grown and that's how I feel. I don't want to be judged, I just want to be respected for my decisions."

"Okay, sis. If that's how you feel, I respect your decision to act brand new."

"So you think that I'm acting like Eve now, too?" I asked.

"I mean, you're definitely doing a lot of the things that she did before she left us."

"I'm not going to start prostituting and I'm definitely not going to kill somebody, Hannah."

"Eve probably said the same things before she did both of them."

"Whatever. What did you cook for dinner? I'm hungry and I smell food." I went to the stove and lifted one of the tops to see what was inside.

"Chicken alfredo."

"Ooo I want some."

"Go ahead and fix me a plate, too."

I fixed our plates, sat on the couch and ate dinner with my big sister. We binge-watched a few episodes of Master Chef. We laughed and talked for hours. I was so glad that I stopped by. I needed to know at least one person I love still loves me and hasn't left or forsaken me yet.

After leaving Hannah's house I went straight home. I put my phone on the charger, decided not to turn on the TV and did something I haven't done in a while: got on my knees and prayed.

Since I hadn't prayed in so long time, I was down there for a long time. I had all kind of things I needed forgiveness for and I wanted to ask God for His forgiveness while I still had the heart to do so.

Once I finished praying, I showered and crawled into my bed. I lay in the dark looking up at the ceiling. It didn't take long before I felt tears falling from my eyes.

I thought about the conversation I had with my sister. I appreciate that she's concerned about me but I'll be okay. I won't let my life turn into what my mother's life turned into. I know what I'm doing. I got this.

Ten

"Tamar Hall."

"Sasha Jones."

"What are you doing tonight?" she asked.

"Um, I don't know. I don't really have any plans. What's up?"

"Lucas wants to hit up the City. You should call Devin and see if he wants to hang out."

"Hit up the City?"

"Yeah, go to a club, get something to eat. You know, turn up!"

"Um, okay."

"Yeah so call your boo and see if he wants to roll."

"Okay. I'll call him."

"Let's go to lunch at noon. I'm starving."

"Me, too. I'll meet you in the lobby at noon."

"Kay, see you later."

Sasha strutted back to her side of the wing and I called Devin. I was hoping that he wouldn't answer or wouldn't want to go out. Going to a club was the last thing I wanted to do, especially since I've never been to one. I didn't have the guts to tell Sasha I've never been to a club before. Nope, I'm not going. I'll just tell Sasha Devin is busy. Yeah, that's what I'll do. Before I could disconnect the call Devin answered. Dang!

"Hey, beautiful, how are you?" he asked.

"I'm good. How are you?"

"Pretty good, busy. What's up with you?"

"Just working, I was calling to see if you were free tonight. Lucas and Sasha invited us to hang out with them tonight."

"Sounds good to me, we can do that."

"Cool. Call me when you're done working. I should know in more detail by then what we're doing."

"Talk to you soon."

I hung up the phone and sighed. Great. Now I have to figure out how to hit up the City, as Sasha says. I have never hit up the City the way Sasha has. My version of hitting up the City is going to dinner and a play. If Hannah knew I had plans to go to a club to turn up, she would come to my job and lay hands on me. Yeah, this one I'll be keeping to myself.

Noon finally arrived and Sasha and I went out to lunch. I told Sasha that Devin and I would join her and Lucas tonight. She was so excited. I tried to join in on her excitement but I was nervous. I've never been into clubbing so I can't exactly get excited. I wasn't sure how I was supposed to dress or what to expect. I've heard stories and going clubbing didn't sound like much fun to me.

I surprised myself by sharing my concerns about my having never gone to a club and not knowing what to wear. After Sasha laughed at me, she agreed to come over and help me find something club friendly to wear. I mean, I've seen how women usually dress when they go out to the City, but I wasn't ready to dress like that. It took me long enough to get comfortable in the dresses I wear to work. I'm definitely not ready to rock the outfits I've seen women wear in the City on a Friday night.

Now that I let Sasha know the truth and she didn't tease me to the point where I didn't want to go out, I was kind of excited. I finally get to see for myself what turning up was really like.

After work Sasha came to my house to search my closet for something to wear. I opened a bottle of Moscato, turned to the Drake station on Pandora and we played dress up. Sasha stretched out across my bed and gave me her fashionista opinions on the outfits I tried on. We finally agreed on a black midi dress that was low cut in the front and hugged every curve on my body. This is one of the dresses Sasha picked out from our last shopping spree sponsored by Richard. I'll be wearing it when we go out of town the following week. I put on a pair of red pumps to bring the outfit together. Sasha was jumping up and down on my bed screaming 'Yes, doll, yes'. I was flattered that my girl thought I looked hot. I didn't want her to know that, so instead I rolled my eyes, shook my head and put my sweats and tank top back on. I poured me and Sasha another glass of wine and sat crossed-legged on my floor.

"Devin is going to be all over you when he sees you. That dress is everything."

"You think so?"

"Yes, doll, he is. You have the cutest shape. I can't believe you used to cover it up in those Ross get ups."

We laughed and I playfully told Sasha to. "Shut up."

"I'm just saying."

"Mmm hmm. So things are getting serious with you and Lucas I see."

"Not really. We just like to have fun. You know I don't take these fools too serious. Not my style."

"I see."

"And what does that mean?" she asked, throwing a pillow at me.

"Just what I said, heffa."

"Look who's calling me a heffa. I see you turning into a ratchet heffa like me. I like!"

"Whatever."

"Okay." Sasha finished her glass of wine. "I gotta go. I need to go home and see what I'm wearing. Lucas is going to pick you up. Have you talked to Devin?"

"Yeah, he'll be here at eight."

"Naughty time before we hit the streets?" she asked, raising her eyebrows up and down.

"No, you thot! We're just going to hang out until Lucas comes, relax."

"Okay, miss goody two shoes. We'll be here around nine-thirty. Try to be off of your knees by then."

"Get out!"

I chased Sasha to the front door and playfully pinched her. That girl and her mouth are out of control, and mine is getting there. I hear myself using words I'd never thought I'd use in a million years. I have never said 'heffa' or called anyone a 'thot' in my life, but being around Sasha and her potty mouth has me saying all kind of things. The spirit of the Lord definitely does not reside in my soul anymore.

Before I knew it, eight o' clock arrived and Devin was at my door. He brought his clothes and a bottle of wine. I was still lounging in my sweats. I didn't want to be sitting around in my dress for over an hour. I figured I'd just get dressed when I knew Sasha would be on her way.

Devin was in a button up shirt, slacks and a tie. He looked so professional and handsome. I don't know why seeing him in a tie made me want to kiss him but I did.

"Somebody is happy to see me," he said.

"I guess so. I didn't mean to kiss you, I'm sorry."

"Don't be. I liked it."

"Good. Is that wine? I sure could use a glass."

"Rough day?"

"Nope, but it will calm my nerves."

"What? Are you nervous having me here?"

"Yes, yes I am."

"Why is that?"

"Honestly because I'm attracted to you and I don't want to do something that I'm not ready for."

"I see. Well, no pressure so no need to worry about that. Okay?"

I smiled. "Okay."

I opened the wine and we sat on the couch sipping wine and talking about our week until Sasha called saying they were on their way. I shocked myself by asking Devin if he wanted to join me in the shower. It had to be the wine. I'm glad that I sobered up when I saw Devin's naked body. I think I forgot I was a virgin or something. I mean, why did I ask this man to get in the shower with me? I was definitely tripping.

I was so relieved that Devin behaved himself. He helped me wash up, washed himself and got out. I leaned against the wall and let out a sigh. That was way too close. I'm clearly playing with fire and I needed to set the matches down.

When Sasha rapidly buzzed the bell I was putting on my lipstick, sliding my feet into my pumps and locking up my condo. Devin smiled when he saw me dressed and slowly nodded his head in approval while I blushed. Sasha was right. He likes my dress.

"About time! We've been down here forever."

"Hush." I put my hand in Sasha's face. "Hey, Lucas, how you doing?"

"Hey, Tamar. Pretty good and ignore Sasha. We've only been waiting for about five minutes."

"Trust me I am." I stuck my tongue out at Sasha. She playfully rolled her eyes.

"Okay, babe, let's roll! I'm ready to party!" Sasha turned the station to Rick Ross, let her seat back and Lucas pulled off.

The entire night for me was a blur. I have no clue what club we went to. All I know is that we had our own section and the waitress kept bringing us bottles of champagne. I knew that I was pretty drunk because I was all over Devin. In fact, I know that I was drunk because when Devin and I made it back to my place, I did the unthinkable: I gave him my virginity.

I didn't realize what happened until the next morning when I woke up sore. Devin was still sleep when I got up to use the bathroom. I looked around my room for evidence to confirm what I thought and there it was. A condom wrapper was on the nightstand next to Devin. I went back into the bathroom, hopped in the shower and cried. I can't believe I gave my virginity to someone I'm not even in a relationship with.

After I showered, I got dressed and sat in my living room. I couldn't even get back into my bed. I didn't want to face that truth right about now. Being in denial is much, much better for me. I hopped on my laptop, put my earphones on and tuned out the thoughts in my head. I felt a hand touch me and saw Devin standing over me in a pair of sweats and no shirt. My goodness! I forgot how sexy he is. I felt myself slowly look up and lock eyes with him. I guess I didn't feel too bad about giving him my virginity because I was right back in bed with him before I could understand what was going on.

Needless to say, Devin and I spent the entire weekend together doing everything under the sun I've never done. I see why people fornicate. It's the bomb dot com.

Spending my weekend with Devin was pretty amazing. I went to work on Monday with a new walk and new outlook on men. I love, love, love me some men. They are definitely the best thing that God has created. I don't see how women are lesbians. Men are everything.

This week was pretty busy for me so I didn't see much of Devin. I flew down to L.A. with Richard on Wednesday and came back Friday morning. I came straight to the office since Richard had a meeting with Mickey Stuart first thing. I sent Devin a text once I got settled. We made plans to hook up after he got off.

Before my meeting with Mickey, Sasha came to my desk. She looked super cute in a white dress with a thin yellow belt and white, yellow and beige pumps. My girl knows she can dress her butt off.

"Hey! Look at you," I said.

"I'm killing it, right?"

"Yes, ma'am!"

"What's up with you? How was L.A.?" she asked.

"It was great. Closed both deals, Richard took me shopping and now I'm back."

"That's my girl. What you doing tonight? Lucas and I are going to hit up the City again. Wanna roll?"

"I'm going to skip the City tonight. Devin is coming over."

"Mmm hmm, I bet he is."

I laughed and said, "Shut up. Let's do lunch."

"See you at noon."

Sasha went back to her desk and I got prepared for my meeting with Mickey. I was so glad that it wasn't long because I wasn't in the mood for his smart mouth today. After the meeting, Richard told me that I could have the rest of the day off. I went to Sasha's office, had lunch with her and went home. Since I didn't have anything to do, I called Devin to see if he could get away from his office for a few. He worked in Berkeley so he was at my home within ten minutes.

Sasha has definitely rubbed off on me. I would have never thought I'd be having a rendezvous in the middle of the day, but I must admit they are fun.

After Devin left, I hopped in the bath and poured myself a glass of wine. Miriam crossed my mind and I started to call her but decided not to. If she asked me what I'd been up to, I'd have to lie and I'm not in the mood to lie. I guess that's why I haven't answered any of Hannah's calls lately as well. I can't tell her what I've been up to without her judging me, so I'd rather not talk to her at all.

I told myself that I'd go to church on Sunday but my weekend was so busy. After I came home from brunch, all I could do was sleep, wash clothes and prepare for the new week. Friday night Devin came back over, Saturday night I hit up the City with Sasha and Sunday we had brunch at HS Lordship. When I got home I was burnt. Now Monday is here and it's time to get back to the money.

Richard surprised me by being in the office when I got to work. I see that he didn't make his own coffee, though. I shook my head and put on a pot of coffee, after which I sat my purse down and stuck my head in his office.

"Good morning."

"Hey, Tamar, good morning."

"What you doing here so early? Another unexpected meeting?"

"No, I wanted to catch you before you started your day."

"Yeah? Everything okay?" I asked.

"Yep, come in and have a seat."

Richard finished typing before he gave me his undivided attention. He folded his hands and smiled at me. I returned the smile, hesitantly.

"When you first started here, I wasn't sure about you. I didn't think you'd be receptive to my demands for you to change, but you were, and ever since then you have been thriving. So, I came in early to let you know that you're receiving a raise. I'm going to be out of the office this week but I thought you deserved to know sooner rather than later. Congratulations."

"Thank you so much, Richard! I really appreciate that."

"You deserve it."

"Thank you."

"I'm going to be in L.A. this week working on the deals we closed. I'll be in contact via phone and email. I'll still need you to be in the office to handle things for me, but I'll take you out to celebrate when I get back."

"Okay."

"Get out, get to work."

I laughed and went to get Richard's coffee. I called Sasha to see if she was at her desk, but she was in a meeting. I called Hannah and told her I got a raise and she gave me a very dry congratulations. I hung up the phone and reminded myself to never call my sister to tell her anything else about me.

When I told Sasha that I got a raise, she hugged me, told me she was proud of me and made me promise that we'd celebrate after work.

"Did you tell Devin yet?"

"Um, no, not yet."

"You should tell him and invite him to celebrate! We can go to this bar around the corner. They have food, too. We can drink, eat and be merry!"

"You play too much."

"But I'm so serious."

I laughed. "Bye girl. Let me get to work. I'll see you later."

I thought about calling Devin but changed my mind. He ended up texting me and asking how my day was going and I told him. He offered to take me out for drinks so I invited him to hang out with me and Sasha. Since Devin is across the bridge, we ended up meeting him in downtown Oakland. Lucas was busy so he didn't come. Sasha had a few drinks with us and went home. Devin and I hung out a little longer before going back to my place.

The next morning I woke up with the biggest hangover. I was so glad Richard wasn't in the office because I definitely wasn't making it to work at nine. I pulled myself out of bed around eight, checked my phone and was surprised to see a missed call from my grandmother. I brushed my teeth, washed my face and put on a pot of coffee. I called my grandmother back but she didn't answer. I didn't know why she was calling, especially at this hour. I called Hannah to see if everything was okay.

"Morning, is everything okay?" I asked.

"Yeah, why?"

"Grandma called me."

"What did she say?"

"I missed her call but she didn't answer when I called her back."

"Oh, well nothing's wrong, so I guess she was just being a grandmother and calling her wayward granddaughter."

"Yeah, okay, so I'm going to hang up now."

I hung up the phone with my sister and shook my head. That will be the last time I try to deal with my family. I'm tired of the judgement. I see why Eve stayed away.

I put my phone on the charger, got dressed and headed to work. Sasha didn't ride into work with me today, so I had my beats by Dre blasting Trey Songz. The song I was listening to made me think of Devin. I resisted sending him a text. Sasha taught me not to chase a man, let him do the chasing, so I'll wait for him to hit me first. I laughed to myself thinking of the things Sasha told me about men. I've tried a thing or two that she's told me and it works.

I didn't get a chance to finish my coffee at home so I put on a pot when I got to the office. While I was in the kitchenette I ran, into Cynthia and Patricia. I smirked as they looked me up and down. This time, of course, there wasn't anything to laugh about. I wasn't rocking a Ross outfit. It was hard to deny how fly I looked in a gray midi dress from Guess and gray peep-toe ankle boots. Even if they wanted to say something, I gave them a look that said I wish they would. I rolled my eyes at the both of them, poured my coffee and checked my emails. I let out a sigh. Even with Richard being out of the office I had a busy week ahead of me. I see why he gave me a raise. Looks like I'll be working harder.

Two weeks went by before Richard took me out for my congratulatory dinner. Everyone from the office showed up and we had a ball. It started off at some fancy Italian restaurant but we ended up at a karaoke bar. I think I had the best night of my life. Seeing my colleagues drunk and singing along to songs they don't really know was hilarious. That entire weekend for me was awesome. After leaving the karaoke bar with my colleagues, Sasha and I met up with Devin and Lucas. We bar hopped before going our separate ways. I spent most of Saturday morning rolling around with Devin and all Saturday evening partying with Sasha. I forgot it was a three-day weekend until Devin invited me, Sasha and Lucas to a party on Sunday night at his friend's house.

Devin had me at a fly mansion in Walnut Creek partying with NBA players, musicians, lawyers and rich executives. Music was pumping, drinks were flowing and everything else under the sun was too, including me. I had never seen anything like it. There was a live band playing jazz, caterers serving food and wine. I felt like royalty being served food I could barely pronounce. Devin impressed me once again. We danced and partied all night long. I was truly enjoying myself until the reality of who I truly am came to light.

I had to use the bathroom so I left my drink with Sasha and stumbled down the hall and found the bathroom. I washed my hands, touched up my make-up and headed back to the party. As I was headed back to the patio with my friends, I saw a familiar face and froze. I forgot that she catered on the weekends. She was the last person I wanted to see, especially dressed like this.

"Tamar?"

"Miriam?"

"What are you doing here?" She looked me up down. I could see she was disappointed to see me like this.

"I'm with some friends." I pulled my dress down and cleared my throat. "I see you're working." She was dressed in all black like the other caterers.

"Yes, doing honest work, unlike you."

"Excuse me?"

"You heard me."

"You know what? I don't have time for this." I started to walk away but she pulled me back. She put her tray down, grabbed my hands and began praying.

"Father God, I come to Your throne on the behalf of my sister in Christ. I need You to break these worldly chains that are keeping my sister bound. I ask that You please have mercy on her and remove her from the stronghold that is keeping her away from You. I ask that You bind the spirit of Jezebel that has taken up residency in her soul, in the name of Jesus. I pray that You remove her from that job and free her from those who are keeping her away from Your Divine and Holy presence. Remind her that she is the daughter of the King and she is sanctified, righteous and holy. Let her know that all she has to do, Father, is repent and give her life back to You and You will create a new heart and spirit within her. I thank You in advance for delivering Tamar from evil. In Jesus' name, I pray. Amen."

Miriam released my hands, wiped her tears, grabbed her tray and went to towards the kitchen. I felt my face was wet with tears also. I went back into the bathroom, cleaned my face and called myself an Uber. There was no way I could stay at this party. Not like this.

I told Sasha and Devin that I had a family emergency and needed to leave. They both offered to come with me but I declined. I didn't want to have to exaggerate my lie about why I was leaving.

As soon as I got home, I undressed, showered and cried. I sat on the floor, letting the water run over me and I cried my soul out.

I turned my phone off, laid in the dark and thought about Miriam praying for me. I was so embarrassed that she saw me dressed the way that I was. I was so embarrassed that she saw me drunk. I was embarrassed that she said things to God on my behalf that I didn't have the courage to say to Him myself. Not even now. I envied the fact that she still had her relationship with God while mine was now extinct.

I used to be on fire for the Lord. I used to love me some God. Now my fire and my love for God has been smoldered by pride, lust, greed and fornication.

I've never thought I'd be the woman who walked away from God. I never thought I'd be the woman who drank. I never thought I'd be the woman who fornicated. I never thought I'd be the woman who wore tight clothes or high heels or weave or make-up. I never thought that I'd be the woman who didn't go to church or bible study. I never thought I'd become the woman who stopped praying, who stopped giving God glory, but I am.

I was so ashamed of who I'd become. I can't believe I've been treating my family and friends as though they've done something wrong when I'm the one who's in the wrong. I thought about how lost I was and cried myself to sleep.

When I woke up the next morning, I looked in the mirror and barely recognized myself. My face no longer held that youthful glow that people often complemented me on. I no longer looked like a woman of God. I now saw a woman who had become a drunk, party animal and fornicator. I no longer saw a woman of the faith, a pure, holy and sanctified believer. I saw a sinner, a woman who has fallen in love with the world. I have stepped outside of the will and grace of my Heavenly Father. I have left the spiritual realm and have officially become a part of the realm of the flesh. And now I can finally see that I'm in a world of trouble.

I thought my faith and relationship with God was as solid as a rock, but I was so wrong. I stopped feeding my soul the Word of God and lost my connection to God. He removed His Spirit from me a long time ago and I was too caught up in the flesh to realize it. Forgive me Father for I know not what I'm doing.

Please, God. Help me....